DEN OF ANTIQUITY

A COLLECTION OF STEAMPUNK TALES
BY MEMBERS OF THE SCRIBBLERS' DEN

TABLE OF CONTENTS

BRASS AND COAL

JACK TYLER

"HAVE A LOOK AT THIS!" Charles Dexter Braxton trumpeted, storming into the seedy office like a general entering his headquarters, and tossing a week-old copy of the *London Times* on James Collier's rickety desk.

Brass and Coal flee London, the left-column headline declared. *Pair sought on continent.*

It went on to describe a pair of confidence swindlers who had bilked a member of the Royal household out of a substantial colonial development bond. Collier tossed it back on the desk without finishing it.

"S-so what?" he asked his portly associate. "It won't t-t-take them long to tumble to the fact that they're l-l-looking on the wrong continent. We should k-k-keep going west, and g-g-get ourselves really lost."

"And subject ourselves to the tender mercies of the red Indians, and those filthy cowboys? I hardly think so! No, James, my young friend, New York is the perfect place to hide. Why, look around, my boy! Have you ever seen such delightful squalor and confusion? The city sprawls for miles in every direction, and boasts every race and social class. Why, all of Scotland Yard's vaunted detectives couldn't find the Queen's consort himself in this rat's nest."

"We could make a c-c-clean start, Mr. Braxton, in an honest t-t-trade."

5

"An honest trade?" Braxton was incredulous. "What's the matter with the one we've established?"

"Well, n-n-n-nothing, I suppose, but, well, Mr. B-B-Braxton, what exactly is a p-p-paranormal investigator, anyway?"

"What does it sound like, James? We are detectives who investigate hauntings and possessions."

"B-b-but, the church does that. And anyway, n-n-nobody's ever proved that g-g-ghosts exist."

"It doesn't matter whether they exist, James, there are people who believe in them, and some of those people have money. Money that would ride just as well in our pockets as theirs. Now, what if you believe you're being haunted, and you aren't a churchgoer? Who will you turn to then?"

When Collier declined to answer, Braxton answered himself.

"To us, that's who, to Braxton and Collier, P. I.s. - Paranormal Investigators. You have a problem the police can't solve? Bring it to us, we can solve it!"

"B-b-but there are no such things as ghosts, Mr. B-B-Braxton."

"Making such problems rather easy to solve, wouldn't you agree? There are people who believe there are, and if we can bring them peace of mind, I should imagine that they would be eager to pay for that. You see, James, we aren't swindlers. We're in the peace of mind business."

The well-dressed, expertly coifed woman, nay, lady, moved along the dimly lit hallway, feeling the grime of ages crunch beneath her elegant shoes. There was an undertone of menace in the nearly deserted brownstone, and she considered retracing her steps and fleeing the area.

Women die in places like this, the little voice of reason whispered in her ear. *Die, and far worse!*

But what she did was for her dear husband, and fear could not be allowed to spoil his chance for safety. So she continued along the gritty hallway, past office after office, most vacated, all dingy, looking for the names her dear friend Agnes had shown her in the Gazette. And at last she found it, its letters glowing in fresh paint against frosted glass yellowed with time:

Braxton & Collier, P.I.

She started to knock, then squared her shoulders and turned the knob. She stepped into an office that made the hallway look inviting, and for a moment she nearly thought that the investigators had moved on since they had placed their advertisement. An unoccupied reception desk stood in the center of the room, covered by a layer of dust nearly sufficient to grow potatoes. The bookshelves behind housed only spiders, diligently stringing their gossamer nets in their efforts to subdue the fly population. Again, she was impelled by a desperate desire to turn and leave, but reminded herself that this journey was about Atherton, and couldn't be abandoned. Hearing then a muffled voice speaking behind the closed door to her right, she gathered her courage, stepped up to it, and knocked, three sharp raps.

The voice stopped speaking, and a moment later, the door was opened by a tubby little man, comical in a suit with waistcoat, barely more than an inch taller than her. He was apparently as surprised to see a lady in these surrounds as she was to be here, and stood gawking at her for a moment.

"Forgive me, sir," she said, "but do I have the honor of addressing Mister Braxton or Mister Collier?"

"Why yes, yes you do."

The man stepped back from the door and waved her into the room with a bow.

"Do come in. I'm Charles Braxton, and this is my colleague, James Collier."

A tall, gangly gentleman with rumpled clothes and rumpled hair rose behind his dilapidated desk.

"P-p-p-pleased to meet you."

"And you are the paranormal investigators?"

"We are," Charles Braxton replied, taking out his handkerchief to dust the seat of a visitor's chair. "Please, dear lady, take a seat and tell us what brings you to our humble place of business."

She hung the crook of her parasol on the back of the still-dusty chair, and mentally abandoning any hope of ever getting her maroon satin walking dress clean again, lowered herself gracefully onto the seat.

"My name is Marigold Reese-Pennington. My husband is Atherton Pennington, who until recently was the junior partner in McHenry, Ltd., a quite successful import firm here in the city."

"Was, Mrs. Reese-Pennington?"

"Please, call me Marigold. My husband was the partner of Phillip McHenry, who was loud and boorish, and treated Atherton abysmally, but he was a wizard of business, and the firm thrived. Last Christmas, Christmas Eve, in fact, on the night of the company's Christmas party, Mr. McHenry took ill and died."

"Unexpectedly?"

"Quite. He was only, well, he hadn't yet reached forty years of age. His doctor said it was a heart attack brought on by gross overindulgence. It doesn't surprise me, mind. Phillip McHenry was a man of vast appetites in many areas, if you take my meaning, and the party was awash in myriad confections, cured meats, and several forms of alcohol. It wouldn't have been difficult for a determined man to commit suicide by food and drink that night."

"No, I suppose not. But pray, Milady, how do paranormal investigators figure into this most tragic event?"

"Mr. McHenry is haunting my husband."

"Really?"

"With God as my witness, Mr. Braxton, his specter comes to him in the evenings when he has repaired to his den to read the papers."

"You've seen this apparition?"

"No, it only appears to Atherton, but I've heard him screaming epithets at it, and his side of a conversation. Only he can hear the other. Mr. McHenry treated my husband abominably in life, and now he's reaching out from the grave to continue his abuse, well, forever, as nearly as I can see. My poor husband has taken to drink for succor. That's why I've come to you. This cannot be allowed to continue."

"No, of course not. When can we visit the premises?"

"At your earliest convenience, of course."

"And is your husband in favor of your retention of our firm?"

"I've told him what I intend to do. He doesn't imagine you'll be of any help, but he has agreed that you may be consulted."

"Splendid. Might we visit, say, just after the luncheon hour?"

"That would be perfect."

"Excellent. What is the address, then?"

"Twelve two-twenty-seven Fifth Avenue. It's a two-story, fronts on the Park. Any cabbie will know where it is."

"Delightful, my dear." He took her elbow to assist her in rising. "Just let us take care of a couple of pressing matters, and we'll be right along. James, escort our client to her conveyance, won't you?"

"Certainly, sir." He extended his arm. "Th-th-this way, Milady."

When Collier returned, having seen the lady into a cab, Braxton was at the window looking out over the city, fairly rocking back and forth with glee.

"Can you imagine it, James?" he greeted his protégé, "A Fifth Avenue address, and our first client!"

"Why d-d-didn't we just go w-w-with her?"

"Never look desperate, James, have I taught you nothing? A Fifth Avenue address. Why, the cost of that dress she was wearing would buy a month's lodging. I have a feeling, my friend, that we have stumbled into a most lucrative line of work!

Messrs. Braxton and Collier began to sort through the collection of odd, non-functional junk they kept crammed into the closet of the second office the moment their client was out of sight.

"It's most important that we look like we know what we're doing," Braxton instructed his partner. "Second most important is ease of transport."

"Ease of—"

"We'll have to carry all this about, load it and unload it, so it can't weigh half an imperial ton, nor can it be too large to fit within a cab. With us, need I add?"

"N-n-no, of course not."

A color wheel attached to a gramophone motor became a "ghost detector," and a cartridge of compressed carbon dioxide, with its impressive rush of white gas, would make an effective "weapon" against a vengeful spirit. It took some doing, but the mechanically inclined Collier managed to conceal it inside a short brass pipe, attach a spring-loaded needle to puncture the neck, and attach an old pistol grip. If the light wasn't too good, it should pass muster nicely. A high voltage travelling arc display, erstwhile known as a "Jacob's ladder," rounded out their "detection equipment," and space was made in their two battered suitcases for the lot.

"These l-l-look awfully shoddy," Collier complained, casting a critical eye on them.

"Nonsense," Braxton dismissed his concern. "That look says that we've been doing this for years! Nothing instills confidence in a mark like the appearance of longevity. These Americans have only had a country for a hundred years or so. When they deal with Englishmen, who have been a nation for a thousand, they expect to smell the mustiness of permanence."

And so the field equipment of the ghost hunters, who didn't believe the first word of any ghost story, was assembled, each of the tinkerer's concerns dismissed, point by point, by the orator. Once assembled and made as professional looking as was possible given their circumstances, they summoned a cab, loaded it up, and set out for the address provided. It was a lovely spring day, crisp and clear, and the two self-appointed experts on the paranormal rode in the plush back seat of the high steam carriage, enjoying the view of Central Park, the "forest within the city."

"I like this neighborhood," Braxton said to Collier, paying as much attention to the houses opposite the park as to the greenery itself. "It fairly reeks of money."

"That's m-m-most certainly so, Mr. Braxton."

"And not old money," Braxton went on. "Old money is old money because the owners know how to hold onto it. No, this street has the feel of people who have just come into it, and feel a delightful compulsion to spend it, none too carefully, at that. Just the sort of people I like!"

"So, wh-what we gonna do at the house?"

"Ah, good you asked. Let's see, what would someone do if they believed in all this hooey?"

"F-f-f-find out all they c-c-could about the ghost," Collier suggested.

"Capital, James! An interview, then. Where have you seen it, how often does it come, and so on. Then get them to commit to using our professional expertise to relieve them of their, mmm, infestation. Take their money, set up our gear, make some strange noises in the middle of the night, and pronounce the haunting at an end. And since there are no such things as hauntings to begin with, we've a foolproof defense should we ever be accused of anything. Why, I do believe we could make a career of this, James. As long as there are stupid people in the world, there'll be no shortage of jobs, what?"

"Here we are, gents," the cabbie said, stopping the vehicle opposite a white-columned, red brick two story with a wide balcony above the door, "twelve two-twenty-seven Fifth. That'll be three-fifty."

"Oh, I like the look of this," Braxton said, counting out the money. "I shouldn't be surprised if the door was answered by a butler. Thank you, my good fellow, and a quarter for your trouble. Let's get our gear, Mr. Collier. We have work to do."

Braxton and Collier walked up the three broad steps to the portico, taking in the spotless paint and the wicker outdoor furniture.

"Delightful aroma, money," Braxton observed. "We'll have to have some cards printed if we're going to deal with this sort of clientele."

"There's n-n-no knocker," Collier replied.

"Pull the bell rope," Braxton told him, somewhat annoyed.

The rope was duly pulled, and a rich gong sounded somewhere behind the double doors.

"Ah, even sounds like money!"

Footsteps could be heard approaching the door, and it was opened by a thirtyish woman in a maid's uniform.

"May I help you gentlemen?"

"Braxton and Collier to see Mrs. Pennington."

"Have you a card?"

"Not yet. We're newly established."

"Very well. Come in, please. May I take your coats?"

She took their coats from them and hung them in a small closet off the entry. Leading them to an alcove off the front hall, she directed them to a comfortable couch.

"Wait here, please."

"I told you," Braxton said when she rounded the corner. "This place has a delightful *je ne sais quoi* that just lifts the spirits."

"Is that French for m-m-m-money, Mr. Braxton?"

"Very humorous, James. It's French for that certain something by which you recognize the superior class of people. From the veranda, to the doorbell, to the uniformed maid service, everything about this place is just, I don't know, right."

"Good of you to say so, Mr. Braxton."

"Ah, Mrs. Pennington," Braxton said, rising. "We were just saying—"

"Yes, I heard. It's good to be appreciated. Will you come this way, please?"

She led them down a crossing hallway to a room at the front of the house, where a man sat hunched in a large chair facing the park out the large windows they had seen from outside.

"Dear," Mrs. Pennington addressed him, "these are the men who are going to restore your peace of mind."

Braxton nudged Collier, and shot him a knowing look.

The man in the chair stood, turned, and regarded them somewhat vacantly, like he might some flowers that he cared nothing about. His left hand held a saucer, and his right a cup, and it was apparent that if he weren't holding them apart, the resultant clattering would be deafening.

"Ah, your ghost hunters."

"Don't start, dear. You promised to speak with them."

"I apologize, darling. Of course, you're right. Won't you sit down, gentlemen? I'm Atherton Pennington, currently the owner of McHenry, Ltd., at least until my late partner succeeds in killing me. I'm sorry, I've failed to achieve any sort of civility. What might your names be?"

"Not at all, Mr. Pennington. I'm Charles Braxton, and this is my colleague, James Collier."

"Pleased, I'm sure. Have you been in the business long?"

"Not in this country, but we've come over from England, where the houses are old, and the ghosts are older."

"Well, that's encouraging. Do you think you'll be able to help me?"

"As you may know, every case is different, but it has been our experience that every case also has a solution. The crux of the matter is finding it. Suppose you tell us everything that has occurred from the very beginning. Your wife told us that your tormentor died at a Christmas party, was it?"

"Just after, actually. Darling, have Miss Devlin bring a fresh pot of tea, won't you?"

"Of course."

"The first thing you have to understand is that Phillip McHenry was a pig."

"Your wife did bring that up."

Pennington smiled.

"I doubt that so fair a creature could convey Mr. McHenry's porcine nature in any adequate fashion. He had no grace, no manners, no personal habits that set him apart from the creature I so freely compare him to."

"She did say he had appetites."

"Appetites? I tell you, gentlemen, if you served him a meal in your home, you could count yourselves lucky if he didn't eat the plate it was served upon! He was a bully, a braggart, a condescending, mean-spirited jackass who even managed to drive customers away from a business as impersonal as importing."

"Please don't think me crass, Mr. Pennington, but if the business paid for this home, surely it wasn't suffering."

"No, importing is lucrative just at the moment. The demand for European goods is such that even a boor can make a decent living at it. But part of our success involved me smoothing the ruffled feathers of people who had had run-ins with his Lordship."

"He was a lord?"

"No. We just called him that because of his pompous arrogance. A lord! The man was more suited to a log cabin with a dirt floor."

"I think we have the picture now, Mr. Pennington. Why don't you tell us about his death, and the subsequent haunting?"

"Quite. Well, part of McHenry's pig-like persona was the way he could shovel in food, and the Christmas party was no exception. It was a party, you understand, so the food was not the sort served in a formal setting. Ah, thank you, Miss Devin," he said as the maid brought in a tray with a fresh pot of tea and all the accouterments. Mrs. Pennington poured and distributed, and soon everyone was settled with a steaming cup.

"Where was I? Ah, yes. The Christmas party. The food was catered, and consisted of confections and pastries, *hors d'oeuvres,* deviled meat, sausages, that sort of thing. There was alcohol as well. Bourbon, brandy, vodka, you name it. Just bottles and glasses, and every man for himself. Well, McHenry spent the evening shoveling in tidbits like a starving man, and washing each morsel down with a shot of whiskey. I don't need to tell you gentlemen that he was roaring drunk within the first hour. Abominable behavior as well. He tried to get every woman in the firm into bed, not that he wasn't too drunk to menace one had he gotten her there. Sorry, darling."

"It's quite all right, dear," she said, blushing.

"Well, he closed the place up, somehow oozed out to the sidewalk and found a cab, and I presume he went home. His housekeeper found him dead in his bed the next morning. Heart attack caused by overindulgence, his doctor said, and it could hardly have been anything else. I've never seen such a spectacle! I smoothed ruffled feathers, brought back customers he had run off, generally kept the business thriving. Things any normal man should have been grateful for. Of course, McHenry was no normal man by any stretch of the imagination."

"No. Most ghosts have a motive for their hauntings, though. Did you insult his mother, frighten his child, something like that?"

"Never knew any family of his. I can't imagine a woman wedding herself to such a pig, and if he had a wife, he kept her a secret. Probably chained in his basement."

"Difficult to see what he might be after. What about the haunting itself? What form does that take?"

"He comes late at night. After dinner, I like to go into my den and read the evening paper. It's sort of a ritual. Relaxes me, gets me ready to sleep, you see. That's when he appears, a cold cloud of malice hovering over the fireplace. He accuses me of despicable acts, and warns me that I'll be joining him soon."

"What despicable acts? Did you do something to him to make him seek revenge?"

"No. The only thing I can think of might be that I ordered the food for the party, but I didn't force him to eat any of it. I didn't force him to drink a gallon of hard liquor either, for that matter."

"Hmm. Odd, though. When someone reaches out from beyond the grave, it would seem that he should have a powerful motive."

"Well, he doesn't, I can assure you. He's probably tormenting me because no one else could stand the sight of him. My wife seems to feel that you can relieve us of his curse, so I have to ask what form that relief might take."

"Primarily, one has to convince the ghost that he's actually dead, and it's time to move on. What we need to do, I think, is to recreate the conditions of the haunting with you going into the den with the paper, as is your normal routine."

"I- I don't know." Pennington paled visibly at the mere suggestion. "It's too much to bear."

"We would, of course, set up our equipment during the day, and be concealed in the room with you."

"And you could guarantee my safety?"

"Unequivocally."

"You have to do it, dear," his wife encouraged. "You'll never be free of this thing until you face up to it."

"I suppose. And you have absolute faith in this equipment, do you?"

"Absolute. No ghost has yet evaded it, here or in England."

"All right, by God, I'll do it! I'll show you the den. You gentlemen can set up your gear, join us for dinner, and tonight, by all that's Holy, we'll lay a spirit to rest!"

The mantel clock gave a single chime; eleven-thirty, and still no ghost, not that Braxton or Collier expected one. They had put on a great show, measuring angles and setting up the color wheel on their phonograph motor, carbide lantern attached to the frame to shine its strong light through the colored pie-slices as it rotated. It had been duly tested and adjustments made in front of the subject so that he could clearly see the level of expertise involved. Collier was certainly no speaker, but was a gifted tinkerer, and his antics with measuring tape, barometer, and prism were the final touches to convince the client that they were worth every dime of their hundred-dollar fee.

The supper to which they were treated was simple fare, but plentiful and excellently prepared, and after a bit of brief conversation at the dining table, the three men had repaired to the den and taken their positions for the evening. Pennington had seemed at first like he would converse with his contractors well into the night, but they pointed out that the conditions must be replicated as closely as possible, and that included refraining from conversation.

So Pennington had seated himself in the comfortable chair behind his desk while the ghost hunters had removed themselves to a bed of cushions they had placed behind a broad screen. The phonograph was placed to the side where Collier could easily manipulate it, and the harmless CO_2 gun was ready to hand. The two men settled down for a boring evening as the room darkened at the setting sun until Pennington's reading light and the fireplace were the sole illumination.

Braxton and Collier made themselves comfortable on the pillows, occasionally passing some disparaging remark in a muted whisper, but for the most part, simply being bored. There was a moment of amusement shortly after ten, when they heard the distinct sounds of a drawer being opened, and the clink and swirl of a beverage being poured. Neither of them imagined that it might be lemonade. Things had gotten quiet for a half hour, then Pennington had begun to hum drinking ditties. Again, a few humorous remarks, and the hunters had settled in for a night's sleep.

Then had come the eleven-thirty chime, slightly rousing Collier, though no more than that, and now, some moments later, Pennington began to speak with the slurred tongue of a man thoroughly drunk.

"You're a bastard, Phillip, and you've always been a bastard!"

Collier shook Braxton awake, putting a finger to his lips as his partner started to speak.

"You think to have your way with me, but I've a surprise for you this time!"

Collier and Braxton peeped carefully around opposite ends of the screen, neither seeing anything out of the ordinary.

Collier, as quietly as he could, got the carbide lamp started, and tripped the release on the Victrola motor, beginning the rotating display of different colored lights.

"You're a son of a bitch, McHenry, and I'm glad I killed you!"

Braxton and Collier turned to one another, wide-eyed, each asking the same question of the other with his eyebrows.

"That's right, you bastard, you're dead! My friends say you don't know that, and as soon as you find out, you have to go on to hell where you belong! What do you think of that, eh? Pretty fix for you, isn't it?"

"He k-killed him?" Collier whispered.

Shhh! Braxton replied.

"You deserved it, Phillip, always treating everyone like scum! I did the world a favor, and not even you can deny it! Now my friends will lay your ghost low, and even the afterlife will have seen the last of you!"

"Charles!" Collier whispered intensely.

"Quiet!" Braxton snapped.

But as Braxton turned his head briefly to admonish his partner, he caught a glimpse in the passing green light, a shape like a bulky form, a small head-like protrusion at the top. Then the yellow lens came into line with the light, and it was gone.

"Stay back!" Pennington shouted. "Stay back, I say!"

He started to step around the desk, reaching for the fireplace poker, then stopped with a strangled scream and staggered back, hands coming up to ward off something only he could see. Braxton, still motivated only by earning his money, and with proper gratitude, a bonus, seized the CO_2 gun, and charged into the room.

"I'll save you, Pennington," he shouted, firing the useless weapon, still believing that all Pennington was seeing were his own delirium tremens. As the cloud exploded into the room, he saw it again, that bulbous, almost man-shaped blob, this time advancing on Pennington in a quick float. Then the dark blue lens came into line, and it was gone once more.

It wasn't gone for Pennington, though. The man cowered, screaming, raised hands waving in front of him before he jerked, or was knocked back into the tall, heavy bookcase behind the desk. As he caromed off, falling across the desk, the heavy piece of furniture rocked, tilted, then came crashing down across his back, heavy volumes pelting him, and driving Braxton back away from him.

All, then, was quiet once more.

"James, get some lights on," Braxton snapped, finally able to rush forward. The bookcase lay on Pennington's back, and when Braxton tried to lift it, it wouldn't budge. "James!"

His partner joined him, and between them they had barely gotten it up when a gasp from the door signaled the arrival of Mrs. Pennington.

"Oh, God, what's happened?"

"Help us lift this," Braxton said, and the three of them were able to move the huge bookcase to the side, and expose Pennington's form.

"What happened?"

"He thought he saw something, recoiled from it, and turned the bookshelves over. Tragic."

Braxton knelt beside him, put a hand on his back, and leaned down to feel for his breath.

"He's still breathing," he announced. "Mrs. Pennington, summon a constable or someone, ask him to send for a doctor."

"Y-y-you saw it, right?" Collier asked as she dashed out the door.

"Saw what, Collier?" Braxton asked, turning Pennington over and loosening his collar.

"The ghost."

"There are no such things as ghosts."

Collier was getting the gas lamps lit, and light was beginning to flood the room. As Braxton lifted the unconscious Pennington into his desk chair, the light glinted off something metallic under the desk. Seeing that the man wouldn't fall over, Braxton bent down to pick up a metal-bound leather case and a folded sheaf of papers. Face below the desk, he saw that it had fallen from a secret compartment that had been jolted open by the impact of the bookshelf. Being both a curious man, and an opportunist, he took the opportunity to open the case. Inside was a vial of an oily orange liquid, a tiny eye dropper, and a ring, its hidden compartment standing open, ready to receive the next filling. He unfolded the papers, seeing a long, handwritten page, and an invoice showing a very expensive price for a product whose name he didn't recognize. Then he heard Marigold Pennington's footsteps racing toward the room, and quickly refolded them and tossed them on the desk.

Mrs. Pennington arrived, followed closely by a beefy police officer who took everything in at a glance.

"Wot's happened here?" the big Irishman demanded.

"Bookcase fell on this man," Braxton said. "Do you think you might fetch a doctor?"

"My partner's gone for a doctor," the cop answered. "They'll be here any minute. Now, just who is everybody, and what're ye doin' in here at this hour?"

"So you see, M-m-mr. Braxton, the flash of light here bounces off the m-m-mirror at the opposite wall, and any inco-co-corporeal object b-b-between the flash and the m-m-m-mirror leaves an impression on the ph-photographic plate here."

Braxton studied the apparatus. It could theoretically be made as large as necessary, with two components on one side of the space, and the carefully angled mirror on the other.

"James, you're a genius," he pronounced. He still wasn't about to start believing in ghosts, but it was shaping up to look like a lucrative business in which a disgruntled client would have a devil of a time proving fraud.

"Mr. Braxton," Emma, their newly-hired receptionist said as she opened the door, "there's a man here from the police department to see you."

"Police?" Braxton echoed. "What does he want?"

"Just want to have a word about Atherton Pennington," a big man in an ill-fitting suit said, pushing the knob out of her hand, and crowding into the room beside her.

"I'm sorry, sir," she said.

"It's all right. Go on back to work. What can we do for you, Mr. uh—"

"It's detective, actually, Detective Thaddeus Mitchell of the 48th Precinct. It was you who found that secret compartment in his desk, wasn't it?"

"Sort of. I think the impact of the bookshelf knocked it open. I found the contents when I tried to help Mr. Pennington."

"Interesting. Pennington was all heated up about the ghost of his former partner coming to kill him. That was why you were there?"

"That's right. His wife retained us."

"Ah, yes. Charming woman. He certainly had her fooled."

"How's that?"

"Well, she was so deeply in love with him and... Look, did you take the opportunity to read those papers?"

"I glanced at them. Wasn't really time, though. A man's life was in danger, and—"

"Yeah, blah, blah, blah. There was an invoice from a shop that caters to the *Santeria* practitioners who move up from Puerto Rico. It was for a liquid form of poison from an aquatic snail that can paralyze the heart muscles, causing almost instant death. The ring in the case, I suppose you saw?"

"Yes."

"The means of delivery. A few drops delivered unseen into a drink, and *poof,* a manufactured heart attack. Also in the letter was the witch doctor's assurance that the drug would work equally well on women. Apparently, he had asked, you know, because of their different constitutions and hormones, you see."

"Quite."

"So the thought down at headquarters is that he killed his partner, and planned to kill the little woman after waiting a graceful amount of time, but his guilt wouldn't leave him alone, and it created a ghost to torment him. Now, you gentlemen were there to exorcise a ghost. You didn't actually happen to see one, did you?"

"W-well," Collier began.

"No, we did not!" Braxton said firmly. "There were some odd shapes, but the light was dim, and one of our instruments uses lights of changing colors, so there was plenty of opportunity for eyes to play tricks, if you get my drift. We saw no evidence of any actual ghost."

"That's what I wanted to hear. Christ, police work will become just about impossible if we find that ghosts are able to go around trying to murder the living. As it is, we don't think we can send Pennington to the gallows, but he'll certainly be one of the oldest prisoners in Sing Sing before he sees the light of day again. There's just one thing that I don't understand."

"What's that, detective?"

"That bookcase. It must have weighed three hundred pounds with all the books in place. And you say he just backed into it, and it rocked over?"

"That's right."

"I just don't see how that's possible. I mean, you'd have to rock it back and forth several times to finally bring it over. You said it took both of you and Mrs. Pennington to get it off of him, and that was after all the books had fallen out."

"Well, yes."

"Just can't see how one bump, no matter how hard, you see, could have tipped that over."

"Maybe the ghost had something to do with it."

"Maybe so," the detective said dismissively. "Anyway, we got the bastard before he could do any more harm, and the ghost of Phillip McHenry can rest in peace, wherever it happens to be. And, as Pennington's spouse and sole heir, the wife stands to become a very wealthy woman when she takes over the business."

"A good day for all concerned, then?"

"Except Pennington."

"Hardly sounds as though he deserved one."

"No. Well, don't disappear, gentlemen. You'll be needed to testify at the trial. You gentlemen have a nice day, and watch out for vengeful spirits!"

And with that, the detective strolled out into the early spring sunshine.

The son of a navy diver and a professional gambler, Jack Tyler carries on the colorful traditions into which he was born. He joined the service to dodge the draft, sailed a wooden ship in a navy made of steel, and cruised the Orient on the deck of a tanker, and that was all before his 21st birthday. Today a grizzled veteran of 67 years of life, many more things have been added to his resume, all of which combine to form his writing style. Having discovered the fascinating world of goggles, gears, and airships some five years ago, he has found his literary home. As he says, "The freedom to tell any sort of story against the backdrop of almost-history and not-quite technology is just too compelling for me to resist. Anyone who has half the fun reading this that I had writing it is in for a wonderful time indeed!

jackshideout.blogspot.com

An Evening at the Marlon Club as Told by Dr. Horatio Boyle

Kate Philbrick

IT HAS BEEN MY PRACTICE in recent years to avoid so-called gentlemen's clubs, as they invariably turn into something of a Free Clinic for the Pompous once one's credentials are made known. However, I had been invited with annoying regularity to attend the Marlon Club in our city, by Mr. Jasper Thumwaitt, an old friend who one must suppose meant well. It was a Tuesday evening, hot on the heels of a most disturbing adventure endured with my dearest friends, when I thought I would partake in a few quiet hours among relative strangers, to regain the social balance of meaningless banter with those completely unknown to me. A step down from hospital rounds, possibly, but not as sticky with particulars.

I arrived at the club without proper introduction, finding Mr. Thumwaitt absent on holiday, to Philadelphia. I thought this rather odd, for I had my own considerations as to where one may spend a leisurely retreat and Philadelphia was nowhere on this list. However, my name was to be found on a roster at the door, indicating Thumwaitt's foresight, that I might at some point accept his standing invitation.

Several of the members were at supper, and having already dined, I continued to the smoking den where I might find a comfortable chair beside the fire. There were but three other gentlemen present, standing near the book shelves, engaged in conversation, and I felt it would be impudent to intrude. I took a seat as unobtrusively as possible and dared indulge in some brandy as well as a cigar, offered by Blavatsky, the attendant.

After a short while I noticed the conversation broke off abruptly. A new arrival had entered the room, and the others felt obliged to make awkward excuses and depart. This left me alone with the gentleman who made his way to a vacant chair close at hand, joining me by the fireside.

He was a ponderously large fellow, tightly packed into fashionable togs, who fell into his seat more than lowered himself, and immediately called for Blavatsky to fetch him a drink and a light.

I nodded a greeting to the fellow, who seemed to be panting with the effort of having made his way across the room, and thought to save introductions until he had regained his equilibrium and mopped his wide forehead with a silk handkerchief. Blavatsky delivered the requested items, though if the stranger had been of my acquaintance, I might have advised against lighting his smoke until he could breathe properly. He grunted his approval, and once the attendant was assured that we required no further attention, he left the room. I had not noticed at the time that he closed the door in his wake, so careful and quiet had he been.

After several puffs ringed our heads with lazy clouds of gray, the man seemed to have righted himself. Bright green eyes focused on me and something of a welcoming smile came to his broad, clean-shaven face.

"Lawrence Pickering." He spoke and extended a pudgy hand of short plump fingers in my direction. I was obliged to lean forward considerably in order to meet this for a sound shake in greeting.

"Horatio Boyle." I responded, not inclined to divulge my medical qualifications at the moment. I had come for companionable relaxation, and did not wish to color any conversation with a litany of complaints in search of diagnosis, should such disclosure be seen as invitation.

"You are new to the Marlon?"

I recounted that, as noted above, while I am no member of any gentlemen's confederation, I had come in response to a friend's request. When inquiry was made as to who my sponsor on this occasion might be, I informed him that Jasper Thumwaitt had been an acquaintance for many years and had kindly made said offer.

"Thumwaitt, Thumwaitt..." The man pondered the name aloud for a moment until a sudden delightful recognition creased his round cheeks with another smile. "Yes, yes! Interesting fellow. Spoke with him..... last week, it was. Quite loquacious. Mind you, I don't support all that nonsense about Heckleberg's work....."

I was moderately surprised at the mention of Professor Heckleberg's name, as I understood none of his most provocative papers and theories had yet been made public.

"You know the professor?"

"By reputation only. Your associate spoke of him at length, rather a devotee it would seem."

The news did not surprise me entirely, as friend Jasper was of a most active mind and not just a little impressionable when an exciting avenue of research made print in one of the journals espoused by the many universities to which he subscribed. While at the time Heckleberg had yet to formally present a lecture or paper on his specific and recent studies, he had nonetheless shared his thoughts with Thumwaitt, who had likewise mentioned them to me, and, as it would seem, Mr. Pickering. Now, of course, Heckleberg's work is known well enough to prevent my belaboring explanation herein.

I had not yet formulated opinion of the professor's strange new theory of inner earth tribal migration to substantiate my belief that the man was a complete loon, so I listened rather than spoke with Pickering on the subject of Heckleberg's known accomplishments. After some moments of expositing, with a growing excitement akin to mounting anger, my new acquaintance settled back calmly in thought. He seemed to look beyond me now, and when he spoke again, it was in whispered hiss, possibly more to himself than to me.

"Of course, he is no Beebenthal….."

It was a curious name, one that I had heard mentioned but rarely over the course of several years—always in passing and with a certain degree of discretion. I recalled on one occasion I had pressed a casual acquaintance to expound upon the mention, to which be reacted with great affront. Said acquaintance informed me that he had most definitely never uttered the name, and if I was to persist in my demands for explanation, he would have nothing further to do with me. I was never to speak with him again and learned, several months later, that he had perished in a most unfortunate accident involving a vat of molten cheese.

My silence was duly noted by Mr. Pickering, who suddenly drew back to the present and looked at me once again, clear-eyed and smiling between lazy puffs on his glowing cigar.

"Stuff and nonsense, all of it. I'm sorry, Boyle, what was it you said of your profession?"

As I deliberately hadn't said a word of my profession previously, I felt it was as good a diversion as any to resume conversation. I explained in light terms how I operated a small medical practice from my home and consulted on cases at hospital. He nodded with appropriate polite interjections, and then asked how Thumwaitt and I had become friends. It was hardly a subject to occupy a moment or two of discourse, at which time I felt it was only reciprocal to inquire after his own circumstances. I elected an open approach, not to assume Pickering was of any particular profession.

"And may I ask how you occupy your time?"

"Me?" He had been listening with eyes half closed and now they shot open wide, as if awakened too soon from a dream. "I eat, man!"

It was not the reply I had anticipated, and the sharp way he had spoken these few simple words made me feel as if I had transgressed. In my speechless pause, I blinked to clear what must have been an error my sight. It had appeared to me that his right eye had bulged most noticeably following his pronouncement—not merely from surprise or rage but unnaturally enlarged beyond lid and hollow as if some macabre bubble. This was so brief as to cause me to doubt its occurrence at all, for within my blink it had arighted itself and regained normal size and condition.

Pickering coughed slightly, his lips concealed by the back of his hand, and then went back to his smoke and brandy as if the preceding few moments had never transpired. It was about this time I thought I heard muffled voices in the hall. These were likewise quick in passing, and only in turning my head did I realize the door had been closed.

Excusing the matter which had caused me momentary alarm, I returned to my own drink and allowed the fire's warmth to lull me to a more comfortable state. Pickering resumed conversation, laconically pointing out his stay at the club to be but temporary. It was at this point I thought I noticed a strange rippling in the flesh of his meaty hands. It must have been an illusion, certainly, due to the relaxing heat and mellowing brandy, or the sting of smoke in the air; as a doctor I knew without question a man's flesh simply did not behave in this manner.

"Have you family?"

My companion's inquiry begged reply and I spoke of my sister, and closest friends. He nodded, the flesh of his face now appearing to ripple as well.

Naturally, I was at this point concerned that I had suddenly taken ill, an acute fever perhaps causing hallucinations. His eye bulged again, rolled wildly and resettled, not completely into its normal position this time. I was determined not to give any hint of apprehension, thinking I should depart and return home before further mysterious delirium could assail me.

There were additional sounds from the corridor now, a heavy bump and some foot-scraping. I looked around again, the door still blocking view of any outside activity, and then noted all else in the room seemed perfectly normal, unaffected by my delusions. I turned back to Pickering when I heard him mumbling.

Once more I found myself blinking, in an attempt to clear my vision. The man's lips seemed to have swollen noticeably, gone from two thin and expressive pink lines to wide, bulbous red slabs of fat resembling unnaturally large earthworms. They glistened with moisture as he continued to mumble, his second eye now growing in size as the first. I confess, it was difficult at this point to conceal my distress and I set aside my glass and cigar with intent to make apologies and rapidly depart.

"…matter…Boyle?" was all I could discern from his speech.

"I must apologize. I am afraid I'm not feeling well." This was not a complete fabrication. "Perhaps the Brandy?" It was from more than courtesy that I inquired, "Are you……alright?"

"Certainly." His voice was thicker now, bubbling from lips that barely parted when he spoke.

He drew a frightful, wheezing breath, and when he raised his cigar for another draw, I observed his fingers had grown oddly in length, darkening at the tips. Had I not witnessed things of such exceedingly terrible nature on that unfortunate recent adventure, I would have bolted screaming for the door. There was another wheezing breath and the distinct but brief sound of fabric tearing.

"What was that?" I spoke by means of distraction.

"Nothing, nothing, Doctor." I was assured without feeling the slightest comfort. His chair creaked as he shifted position slightly. Convinced now that I was most certainly witnessing something beyond the norm, and was perhaps in some peril, I pushed myself up from my chair.

"I'm afraid I really must be going."

These words had hardly been pronounced when something caught me about the ankles, pulling my feet forward and out from under. I fell roughly back into the chair and glanced down in time to see a thick dark tendril slithering across the carpet. I mistook this in the instant for a snake, despite the fact it was extending from Pickering's trouser cuff.

"…Must….stay, Boyle." He croaked through blubbering lips now thick with blue spittle. The black edge of a pointed tongue darted across his lip, followed by the hiss, "…….not….at all….Beebenthal…."

A clattering of noise rose behind me now from the hall.

"I say, some assistance here, please!" I called out in hopes of being heard.

Something wet now pressed against my chest—which I can only describe as the slimy appendage of an octopus or squid, originating from the torn waistcoat of my companion. All thought of polite behavior under these circumstances fled in an instant.

Pickering stiffened, gasped and opened a hideous maw as his body trembled violently, bursting his clothes at the seams. Fighting panic with no great success, I pushed violently against the floor in a bid to overturn my chair and escape the slithering reach of tentacles. The door crashed open bringing a rush of angry voices as I flew backward and struck my head. The world went black, sparing me sight of the mayhem to follow.

I am embarrassed to admit I do not know how long I was incapacitated by the blow to my head, though I felt it could not have been more than a few moments. I opened my eyes and rolled out of my fallen chair with less grace than urgency. The room was full with a disturbing mix of odors, too foul to bear description. Furniture was overturned, and a curious bluish-green substance akin to an oily slime dripped here and there from various points to puddle on the floor. The carpet was pushed and rolled askew, torn and bearing evidence of a great struggle. Oddly enough, the fire in the grill flared and sparked as if nothing was any different from the moment I had arrived.

Pickering's chair was unoccupied, turned away to one side, its seat singed and smoldering and the arms torn away. I found my feet as quickly as possible, unsteady enough to need support from a side table. This too was spattered with the blue oily ooze that seemed to hiss, bubble and sizzle unnaturally against the wood.

Somewhere within the club, down the corridor and in rooms beyond, came the muted sounds of shouting, and the smashing of wood and glass. There were other noises as well, as pistols discharged and rumbling growls rose shuddering in objection. I dared not put to mind possibilities of what had transpired, or was indeed still running its course, and feeling dazed from my injury, moved toward the open door.

I beg the reader will not mistake my actions for cowardice, but I admit to exercising the better part of valor in flight. I departed the Marlon Club with haste, a shower of glass dashing the walk behind me from an upper window as I did so. By the time I had reached the boulevard, several constables came rushing past, with the din from the Marlon fading slowly as I progressed.

Not long after, the Daily Fredonian had a small reference, page 5, column 3, of recent structural damage to the Marlon Club incurred during repairs. There followed, perhaps two days later, a post from the Marlon, with profuse apologies for the unfortunate incident which had marred my visit. No mention was made specifically regarding Pickering, excepting that the club was to soon modify their regulations in reference to courtesies extended visiting members of other organizations. I was thanked for my discretion, and subsequently offered membership for life, among other gestures of gratitude.

In light of the experience, I am afraid I shall have to decline.

Kate Philbrick (aka Mrs. Emeline Warren) writes mainly historic adventure & horror to amuse herself and friends (don't laugh! That's how the Brontes started!) Her novel Unburied Dead landed her the job of editing Richard O'Brien's auto-biography (unpublished). Her non-fiction work appeared in teen magazines in the '70s, and she has written and edited newsletters for various historical groups. She is on the staff of Weird NJ magazine, with works appearing in both WNJ books, as well as their regular and special issues. Current fiction projects include the Mudlark, a Victorian murder mystery and the Steampunk series Ashlands.

Dragon's Breath

E.C. Jarvis

Part 1 – Stoker

Wind whistled through the cab of the locomotive, pushing the loose strands of Mud's hair across his face, sticking them to his beard. He puffed them away with a breath out of habit. They would turn in a mile or two and the wind wouldn't whip so hard from that direction, no need to adjust his cap for that.

"More," the engineer, Harrold, called to him.

Mud flipped open the firebox, heat roaring from within, singeing his already blackened face. He jabbed his shovel into the coal and lobbed a few loads into the fire checking the water level as he went.

"More," Harrold said again. They had been going for two hours and though Mud usually preferred a silent trip, Harrold had only said two words to him for the entire journey, *more* and *enough*.

"Enough," Harrold said once Mud had shovelled a few more loads into the firebox. Mud chewed on his teeth. He was an experienced fireman, knew damn well when more was needed and when enough was enough, he kept his mind sharp and his tools sharper. Harrold had succeeded in pissing him off, making him feel like a teenage boy who didn't know a thing. The one thing he did know for sure was that punching his engineer in the nose would get him the sack and getting the sack from this job – as odd as it was – would guarantee he'd never work again. So he leaned his chin against the handle of his upturned shovel squishing his beard, stared out at the landscape as it flashed past sideways, and reminded himself over and over not to punch Harrold, no matter what.

The locomotive turned on the tracks, though not to the West as Mud had expected, they passed to the East, the wind curling through the cab harder as they turned into the path of the impending storm. He opened his mouth to speak, to ask where they were headed, or question the change of direction, and then snapped his mouth shut. He knew there would be no answer for that question. He was there to shovel coal, nothing more.

Mud adjusted his cap, tucking his long black strands of wayward hair underneath the faded material.

"Change of plan," Harrold called back to him without turning to look as he tugged on the brake to slow for another bend in the track.

"Right," Mud yelled. He had the feeling that Harrold wanted him to ask why, seeing as he hadn't struck up a conversation until now, but he wasn't about to play up to him.

"New destination," Harrold continued, "more." He turned and gestured to the firebox giving Mud a pointed stare. A tunnel approached in the hillside ahead, masked by a thick blanket of tall evergreens. The tracks had begun to climb up the steep hill, the engine of the steamer chugging slower with the adjusted angle. They were in a rush to make time. Mud shovelled more loads, his thick arms not minding the extra work out though he was used to driving at a slower pace with the union, this private job was a different matter. Losing speed on this journey was not an option. That's why he'd been chosen, his ability to work fast and keep his mouth shut was all they had wanted, and offered a handsome pay in return.

As he slammed the firebox shut, he pulled a grubby pocket watch from his shirt pocket and checked the time, moments before the train was plunged into the darkness of the tunnel. They had another ten minutes till their scheduled arrival time, though now the direction of the locomotive had switched he really had no idea where they were going. This section of track was unknown to him. Private land, tracks unused for all he knew.

They emerged at the peak of the hill, the track curved sharply to the North. Harrold tugged on the brake and the wheels screeched as the train slowed. A gust of wind swiped the cap from Mud's head, flinging it straight into the coal pile and sending his long curly hair into a halo dancing around his head. He grunted in frustration and grabbed his cap, scrunching it up in his hand.

The train came to a stop in the middle of the track. There was no station, nor obvious building nearby. One side of the cab opened out to the edge of a chalky white cliff with a sheer drop down to the ocean below, he guessed it to be at least a hundred feet down to the water. The other side dropped out to a grassy knoll surrounded by more tall evergreens.

The engineer stepped down from the cab and disappeared out of sight. Mud rested his chin on the shovel again. It was not his business to intervene nor interfere. He checked his pocket watch again, pushing a layer of soot from the glass face with his equally soot coated thumb. They were ten minutes early. Night was drawing in across the sky over the ocean.

"Muddock," Harrold's voice called on the wind. Mud stuck his head out the door and curled his neck around to look down the length of the train. The three carriages were stopped on a curve, lights from the gas lamps within edging round the drawn black velvet curtains. It looked like some sort of a hearse train. Harrold was stood at the end of the coal car, a handful of men and women had joined him. The men were dressed in dark robes and top hats, one particularly fat man wore a monocle. The women were dressed in sombre black dresses, bustles sticking out at the back. Gentry types. Harrold beckoned for him to come out and he did so reluctantly, trudging along the muddy grass in his heavy boots, dragging his shovel with him.

"Bring your man into the pit," the man with the monocle said to Harrold, his voice laced with haughty tones, he pulled a long thick chain from a bag. "You and he can follow at the back of our group. I'm not having him stay with the train by himself, the last man we had got spooked and tried to drive himself away leaving us stranded, we had to call for an airship to extract us at great expense. At least try and make yourself look presentable dear fellow. This isn't a commoners place and whatever you see or hear down there you shall never speak of."

With that, the fat man marched on leading through the trees. The others followed, more and more people streaming from the carriages of the train, one or two bringing lanterns with them to light the way. Harrold and Mud followed at the rear as instructed. He looked at the cap in his hand, wondering if putting it back on would do anything to make him look more presentable and then instantly discounted the idea. He was covered in soot, arms and face black, clothing tattered, short of taking a swim in the ocean and stripping nude, he could do nothing to change his appearance out here. He noticed a few men carrying pistols in their belts and one particularly interesting looking woman had a black leather whip swinging from her hip. Mud found himself both wary and intrigued by the strange group.

He gave the train one last mournful look before the line of trees closed in behind him blocking it out of sight.

PART 2 – THE PIT

"Thirteen steps to the base," Mister Warren Colling called from the front of the line. Sasha clicked her tongue. Their leader had a penchant for the dramatic that she did not share. The thick blanket of trees opened up a little and the light from the lantern bearers shone across the cave opening ahead. She approached the steps with caution wishing again that Warren hadn't insisted on her wearing high-heeled boots. Navigating the narrow steps in the chalky stone would have been tricky enough in flats. She tapped the whip at her side, checking it for the hundredth time since they'd set out.

Something burned into the back of her neck as she descended into the cave and she gave one last glance backwards before the ground blocked her view. At the back of the queue of people stood the engineer and fireman his blackened face curtained by a head full of black hair and a bushy black beard. She knew why Warren had made them come along, but they did not belong, and the way the fireman's bright eyes locked onto her sent a shudder down her spine. Did no-one else question their presence here?

As they moved further into the cave her thoughts moved from the questionable new members and her fingers twitched beside the whip. Her role would come into play soon. It was a wonder that Warren didn't make her walk at the front of the group instead of somewhere at the back. That was the way of the Order, no-one moved up in rank until they had proven themselves worthy and for all the times she'd done so, she'd shot herself in the foot by being sarcastic or ungracious. Such traits were not desirable for one of higher rank. At least she wasn't likely to be called upon for sacrifice. She looked back toward the fireman and engineer again, surely they would be needed for the return journey? How would their silence be assured?

They came to large opening and the group spread out along the ledge that ran around the side of the pit below. Warren adjusted his monocle with his right hand while gesturing for her to join him in the centre of the pit with his left hand. She traversed the last of the steps and then leapt down the gap into the pit. The lantern bearers lit the braziers around the edge of the pit, giving light all around. The last patch of sky above had turned navy blue with night's approach.

"You know what to do Sasha," Warren said loudly enough for everyone to hear. "Try to be graceful this time," he whispered into her ear, and then headed to the large iron gate that was built into an opening in the rock. He pulled out a large key from his pocket and turned it in the padlock, then swung the gate open, trapping himself against the wall behind the gate, his podgy belly sticking through the bars.

Sasha pulled the whip from her belt and stretched it out as she took up her position in the centre of the pit. She felt the eyes of those watching tingling on the back of her neck as she awaited the arrival.

From within the darkness ahead a low growl emerged. Sasha braced her feet, digging heels into the dusty dirt as if she could anchor herself to the spot. A pair of silver eyes appeared, moving low to the ground, ready to pounce. Sasha loosened her grip on the whip, stretched her arm out to the side. The creature emerged from the shadows. The men around the ledge of the pit readied their pistols. Sasha raised her free arm and waved to them to stand down, spooking it with gunfire wouldn't help the situation at all.

Thick black paws landed softly on the dusty ground as the creature padded towards Sasha its head bent low, sharp teeth bared in its maw, a spark of silver around its neck. A pair of black wings unfurled from the long black body and flapped onto the ground reaching both ends of the pit. The creature growled, locking eyes with Sasha. She curled the whip round, it cracked in the air above the head and the creature bowed, ducking away from the sound.

Warren peeked out from behind the gate, lobbed a length of chain out into the pit. His throw was short, the chain landing between Sasha and the dragon. She clicked her tongue and forced herself not to roll her eyes.

Sasha stepped forward. The dragon's eyes never left her face as she moved toward the chain, slowly, softly, keeping grace in mind.

A flash of movement to the side caught her eye. The dragon spun and ducked to the ground, turning its attention sideward. Sasha cracked the whip in the air, trying to draw its attention back to her, to no avail. Someone had joined her in the pit, to her shock she saw the fireman stood, legs splayed wide, shovel raised above his head as though it were a battle-axe.

"Stop!" she yelled to the man, but it was too late. The dragon reared up on its hind legs, exposing the belly, a red glow burgeoning in its breast the light shaped as scales and cogs. The fireman seemed to understand what was coming as his white eyes grew round and he swung the blade of the shovel in front of his face. A shot of flame erupted from the black monster, precisely aimed at the fireman's head. The fire shot around the sides of the shovel. A woman on the ledge of the pit screamed as the deflected flame caught her skirts setting them alight.

"Alhanra," Sasha screeched as she cracked the whip down onto the dragon's back. It bucked and turned, the flame dying down as the dragon beat its wings. Sasha whipped again, catching one of the wings, refusing to panic in the face of utter disaster. By the third crack of the whip it seemed it was too late as the dragon prepared to take flight. Another flash to the side caught Sasha's attention. The fireman rolled forward, shovel in hand, he whirled around to stand upright, smacked the creature across the side of the head causing it to stumble and cry out in pain. The man then bent down to collect the chain, hooking it onto the collar on the dragon's neck, then tossed the other end to her.

She raced to the edge of the pit, hooked the chain into a large pin embedded into the rock and then turned back to face the battered beast.

Warren emerged from behind the gate, looking down at his monocle, the glass smashed. The dragon sidled off to the side of the pit, cowering away from the fireman who stood in the middle, his beard burnt from existence, his skin even blacker than it had been before, but he lived and Sasha wasn't quite sure how.

One thing was for sure, it had not been graceful.

PART 3 – THE DEN

Mud stared at the creature opposite. A dragon.

"What do you think you are doing man?" Warren yelled at him as he marched across the pit.

"More than anyone else," he said, feeling irked again that no-one had thought to jump in and assist the woman before the dragon burnt her to a crisp. As it was, one of the other women on the ledge had succumbed to flame and was writhing her last on the floor of the pit. No-one seemed to care.

"He tamed Alhanra," the woman, Sasha said as she joined them.

"He smacked the dragon with a shovel. I don't think it counts," Warren said with a derisive snort.

"The rules are clear Warren. It doesn't matter how, all that matters it that he has shown mastery. What is your name?" Sasha asked as she turned to face him.

"Mud."

"You don't think I'm going to let a commoner who calls himself Mud, into the inner workings of our sacred order, do you?" Warren said.

"The rules are clear," Sasha repeated.

"No. You can sit out here with him while she eats. The rest of us will go inside."

Warren turned on his heels and marched into the cave entrance. Two men collected the dead woman from where she had fallen and carried her lifeless body over to where the dragon was slumped down at one end of the pit, flinging the body towards it, then scurrying down the tunnel with the rest of them. Only the engineer, Harrold, remained outside with Mud and Sasha. Harrold sat down beside the steps glaring at them in silence.

"You didn't need to jump in you know," Sasha said as she watched the dragon feasting on the charred remains of the victim. "I had her under control."

"With a whip?"

"I am her trainer; it has been my place to tame her since she hatched. You shouldn't be here. I shouldn't be telling you this."

"It wasn't my idea to come out here. I'm just the fireman."

"I know, but you have to realise what will happen to you after... they won't let you live."

Mud stared down at her as she perched against the ledge. He rubbed a hand over his beard and then grunted in frustration as he realised that what little hair remained on his face was scorched, the smell of burnt hair assaulting his nostrils. It was a little too much to take: the dragon, the weird cultists and now the threat of death for simply existing. He was beginning to regret agreeing to the job.

"Last time I take a private contract," he said more to himself than to her he wasn't used to speaking with high society women. She laughed through her nose. Mud stared at the dragon as it gorged on the body, ripping limbs apart with its teeth with the ease of pulling apart a well cooked chicken. Mud knew he should feel disgusted at the sight, but in reality he wasn't bothered. If that poor woman had no-one to mourn her then he wasn't about to volunteer for the task.

"Where did you get picked up from anyway?" Sasha asked.

"Don't matter if I'm about to be dead."

He looked over at Harrold. He could fight the engineer easily enough if needs be and the woman wouldn't be much of a match for him. The dragon might pose a problem though.

"You need a wash," she said, her eyes catching his. She was perfectly clean, not a smudge on her pale skin nor a strand of her long auburn hair out of place from the bun at the back of her head.

"I can die dirty, just as well as you rich folks die clean."

"Is your name really Mud?"

"What does it matter?" He really wasn't used to being asked so many questions.

"It just seems odd."

"And a bunch of cultists convening up a hillside with a pet dragon guarding their cave isn't odd?"

"You won't hear me argue otherwise," she said with a wide smile and sparkling eyes.

"I thought dragons died out long ago," he said with a nod to the creature who had consumed the entire body and was now settling down to lick its paws. It almost looked like a contented dog rather than a fire breathing killer.

"They did. She is a hybrid."

"A hybrid dragon?"

"I'm not sure I should tell you more."

"What does it matter if your friends are going to kill me off?" he said, getting frustrated at the situation. Maybe it would be easier to just smash her and Harrold with the shovel and drive the train away alone, risking the ire of the dragon.

An abrupt scream escaped the mouth of the cave, cutting off any response that Sasha may have given. Mud stood, his toes curling in his boots, and grip tightening on his shovel.

"You shouldn't go down unless you're invited," Sasha warned, placing her hand atop his blackened arm.

"What does it bloody matter?" he barked at her, marching toward the entrance.

"Muddock, enough!" Harrold called to him from across the pit. Mud ignored him and pressed onwards into the dark.

He walked a few paces in darkness and then felt his boots slipping away on uneven ground as the dusty floor crumbled down a slope. He slipped and slid, trying to use the shovel for balance to stop himself tumbling down the slope on his backside. Eventually the tunnel opened and levelled out into a large chamber.

A flash of fire roared up from below, crackling the air with heat and ash then dissipating. Mud slipped down onto his stomach and crawled to the edge of the ledge, peering over. At least fifty feet below there was a large pit, ten times the size of the one outside and there were three dragons chained to the walls. These were far larger than the one outside. Bodies of pure muscle, like bulky oxen, two red and one dark green, wings so large they could not stretch out properly in the space without scraping the walls, and sharp pointed teeth as long as the wheels of a train.

He stared down into the pit – the den – watching the dragons pace. Their movements were not as fluid as he would have expected from a creature of nature, instead their legs seemed rigid, like metal pins moving within joints and as another burst of flame erupted from the green dragon who spread its wings as it roared fire to the other two, the wings shimmered in the light, filled with veins to the tips, where he would have expected to see bone he could have sworn he saw metal bars hinged at the joints beneath the skin of the wing.

"What are you doing?" Sasha whispered as she fell to her belly beside him and peered over the ledge.

"Looking. What are you doing?"

"Trying to keep you out of trouble."

"Someone screamed."

"Another sacrifice." It keeps them happy to have the occasional human to eat instead of sheep and cattle.

"What is this place?" Mud asked.

"It's their Den of our sacred order. We have been working for a hundred years to bring dragons back into the world from a nest of eggs that our founder discovered. Their bodies cannot survive without... adjustments."

Mud looked at Sasha. It sounded like madness. A bunch of people calling themselves a sacred order, keeping pet dragons in a hillside and making mechanical adjustments to the creatures to keep them alive. She seemed to think nothing of it though and it really wasn't his place to ask questions or intervene.

Sasha looked down into the chamber as another blast of fire lit up the cavern. A strand of hair had fallen from her bun and was dangling on the dusty ground and the front of her dress was coated in a layer of dust. If she didn't like dirt then she was about to be in for a shock when she discovered what following his lead would do to her posh attire.

Mud scooted backwards away from the ledge and stood up, out of the view of those below. Leaving would be easy compared to staying. He could get a new job on a merchant steamship in a boiler room and sail away before these people managed to get themselves off the hillside. As he turned he found a group of men, armed with pistols blocking the exit.

PART 4 – FLIGHT

"You were instructed to stay outside," Warren said as he joined the men, resting his arms across his fat stomach, "and as for you, Miss Franklin, this is the very limit of your indiscretions."

"If you kill me, then you'll have no-one to tame Alhanra. She will burn and eat anyone who tries." Sasha stuck her nose in the air, ignoring the vein of terror running down her spine. She wasn't sure if Warren would make good on his threat or not but intended to remind him of what would happen if he killed her. She couldn't vouch for the fireman, Mud. There was something about the strange man that attracted her. He was low-born, common as muck, had a dirty name to suit his dirty appearance, but he had stepped in when he'd thought someone was in danger, at least twice. Such gallant actions were usually reserved for heroes, not men in tattered clothing plastered with a layer of soot. Now his long bushy beard had been burnt off he almost looked handsome underneath the thick covering of long black hair on his head, and the way his eyes seemed bright looking out from the blackness of his face held her attention. She felt safe standing by his side, even when he was only armed with a shovel. As handy as she was with a whip, neither of them could truly fight against pistols.

Mud reached into his shirt pocket, causing the twitchy gunmen to take aim.

"Just checking the time," he said as he scraped a layer of dirt from his pocket watch before dropping it back into the pocket.

"What for?" Warren asked.

"If I'm about to die, I'd like to know the time of my death."

"Odd fellow. So be it," Warren waved a hand to the men at his side. Pistols raised pointing at Mud's chest. Sasha flinched, waiting for the sound of gunfire. Instead, Mud whirled on the spot turning the shovel in his hands into a bat and knocking the pistols out of the men's hands in one swipe. Chaos erupted. A pistol fired, the dragons below roared, the combination of three lots of flame scorching the back of Sasha's neck. She lunged forward, narrowly escaping a set of flailing arms that seemed to be trying to grab her. Mud swung his shovel again, catching one of the men across his face and sending him to the ground. Warren lunged forward and Mud smashed him on the back of the head. The plump man stumbled over the ledge and screamed as shrill as any woman as he tumbled down toward the expectant dragons below.

Sasha felt someone grab her arm and drag her across the dusty floor. It took a moment to register who had her in a vice like grip as she stumbled through the dark tunnel.

"Time to leave," Mud said, dragging her out into the night air.

It was raining, the storm had finally closed in and the dark night sky gave little light to the outer pit. She pulled Mud to a stop as he raced for the steps up. The engineer Harrold was nowhere to be seen. Mud stood, rain drenching his hair and plastering it to the sides of his face, soot running down his skin as it washed away. He cocked his head to one side and motioned to her to be quiet. Back down below they could hear screams and roars of the dragons and people below, but in the other direction a different noise emerged, the sound of a train.

"Bastard," Mud said baring his teeth, "I was looking forward to breaking his nose."

A low growl emerged from the other side of the pit, and Sasha instinctively gripped her whip. Alhanra was bent low, her wings spread out. She was looking directly at Mud, her sparkling silver eyes intent. Sasha reached out to grip his arm, to warn him to back away, but before she could he stepped forward, raising his shovel in the air. She bit her lip, not wanting him to get burnt to a crisp, nor to see the dragon get hurt. Mud turned his shovel in the air and then swung it down with full force as Sasha screamed out.

The shovel smacked into the ground, slicing through the chain as though it were a knife cutting butter. Alhanra straightened her legs and shook the rainwater from her wings, stepping forward to sniff at Mud. Her large nostrils huffed at his shirt in some form of approval and then she bent down once more stretching her wings behind her back.

"I think she likes you," Sasha called to him, not hiding the laughter in her voice.

Mud affixed his cap to his head, swung the shovel across his back, latching it through the braces crossing his back and then offered his hand to her.

"I'll see you home Miss," he said, the rainwater had almost washed his face clean. He really was quite handsome beneath the soot.

"Don't you have an engineer you'd like to pummel first?" she asked as she accepted his hand and they climbed onto Alhanra's back. Sasha felt his arms lock against her side, his chest to her back, the small singed hairs on his chin tickling the crook in her neck. They bent forwards together, lying close across the black dragon's back, knees locked tight around her body.

"Could do. Those private trains are worth a fair price," Mud said.

"Yes, you'll need the money for repairs if Alhanra breaks anything in her body."

"When we're done with the train, we'll come back for the others."

"I'm not sure anyone in the Order survived down there," she said, glancing one last time at the cavern entrance.

"I meant the dragons."

Alhanra beat her wings and leapt into the air, arching up into the storm above. In minutes they cleared the treeline, cold rain pelting against Sasha's skin, hot arms holding her steady. In the dark forest below she could see the locomotive backing up the track slowly, the chugging of the engine confirmation that Harrold had fled. Mud pushed on the dragon's neck to turn her towards the plume of smoke the rose up into the night sky. Alhanra beat her wings, slowly gaining speed.

"More," Mud called as they arced out across the clifftop, the ocean waves crashing into the cliff far below. The simple command was immediately understood as the dragon sped up, racing towards the train.

Somehow, though she was riding on the back of a dragon with a man she barely knew, Sasha felt safer than she'd ever felt before.

As the dragon curled in a spiral toward the train, Mud pulled back, slowing her down.

"Enough," he yelled. The dragon spread out its paws and landed with grace atop one of the carriages. It seemed he would get to punch Harrold in the nose after all.

E.C. Jarvis is a British author working mainly in speculative and fantasy fiction genres. For the last thirteen years, Jarvis has been working her way through the ranks of the accountancy profession in various industries. During ten of those years she has also been writing.

"It was always a hobby. I'd knock a poem out every now and then, or enter something into a short story competition, with very little success, but that never stopped me. There has always been an underlying need to write. It comes and goes with varying intensity, but it's always there, like an itch that needs to be scratched."

Her first success at publishing was a poem in a collection titled Fear Itself published by Forward Poetry in 2012. Following a three year hiatus where she "couldn't even bring myself to write a shopping list", 2015 saw a turnaround that has seen her write a whole bunch of books.

She was born in Surrey, England in 1982. She now resides in Hampshire, England with her daughter and husband.

www.ecjarvis.com
https://www.goodreads.com/author/show/14441226.E_C_Jarvis
https://www.facebook.com/E.C.JarvisAuthor
https://twitter.com/EC_Jarvis

THE RELUCTANT VAMPIRE

NEALE GREEN

WHY WERE THEY SO FRIGHTENED of him? It wasn't as though he fed off them; he hadn't fed off humans in over four hundred years, not since that insane time in the war when he didn't know who or what he was. When he'd looked into it once he'd came to his senses again, he'd determined that that time couldn't have been more than two or three weeks at most. He didn't even feed off their livestock unless he couldn't find a big enough deer or wild boar to feed off, to quench that hunger.

He did curse that creature who had done this to him, that crazed animal that descended on him while he was standing sentry duty on the Janissary camp, back in the campaign against Vlad Dracula. He'd managed to kill it before it did him, just barely, but as it died, everything in it had flooded into him. He hadn't been much better than that creature for those few weeks before he'd managed to wrestle the demons down and regain control of himself though, the way he'd gone into a feeding frenzy whenever that hunger struck like he did.

When he'd come to his senses again, Bilal had sat outside the Janissary camps at night and listened to them talking about how it must be Dracula doing these killings, because everyone knew that he was some kind of devil. He had to laugh at that, to think that he'd only added to the legends about the one they'd come here to defeat. That was hundreds of years ago now, and no trace of those men would remain, but he was still hearing the name of Vlad Dracula.

As well as the creature that had inflicted this on him, Bilal cursed the affliction itself, because while having strength and speed several times that of normal men was useful, having senses many times more acute than normal men was more of a two edged sword. Those senses meant that he could hunt in the night like no other, but they also meant that he couldn't go about in the daylight without the light searing his eyes and feeling as though it was burning his skin.

Bilal had learned to filter out much of the noise that bombarded him in this increasingly noisy world, which was a boon now that his world was full of steam engines chuffing and clanking, and blowing loud whistles, often preceded by men blowing horns to warn of their coming as well, even this far away from the cities. How he missed the world of only a hundred years ago when all you'd hear was men and animals, except in times of war when the muskets and cannons were going off.

He'd also learned to filter out many of the smells of this world, which was again a boon, especially now that those steam engines were commonly burning coal. He could stomach the smell of the wood smoke, the grease that they slapped onto their moving parts, or even the smell of hot metal emanating from their boilers well enough. That dank reek of burning coal that was growing ever more prevalent often left a bad taste in his mouth though.

While he could dampen the noise and the smells of this world to a degree, the sun defeated him, he could not go out in the daylight unprotected. To venture out, he had to wrap cloth over his eyes and pretend to be blind any time he was near people, many thought him a leper too from the way he was covered up. Without these protections the sunlight seared his eyes and burned his skin.

As he watched the light fading, he finished packing what things he had, because even though he needed to hunt, he must move on, as the townsfolk were getting more emboldened about 'hunting down the creature'. They wouldn't find the helpless creature that the legends gave them to expect, but he didn't want to have to kill them merely because they were ignorant and afraid.

When he'd tied up the bundle of his things, he settled it on his back and tightened the ropes. With his bundle secured, he picked up his staff, which also served as a blind stick and spear shaft as required, and tested the air, looked and listened for any sight, sound or smell that might say that people may be about before he headed out.

He'd been loping along for a few hours when he spotted the stag. He could sense the energy in him and knew that this one would sustain him for a while, as would his meat. Bilal stalked closer, but it sensed him when he was still fifty paces away and took off. The beast had no chance of outrunning him though and he ran it down easily, stunning it with a blow to the head. With it dazed, he bit into its neck to interrupt the flow of energy to its head and sucked the life energy out of it (this was the only spot on most creatures where this worked effectively).

The stag struggled, but it couldn't break free of his vice like grip and Bilal sucked at the life energy that coursed through it until it collapsed, spent. When the stag was gone, he reverently thanked him for his sacrifice, then skinned him, butchered him and tied as much of the choicest cuts as he could eat before it spoiled into the skin and added that to the bundle on his back before going on his way, rather more invigorated.

As much as he disliked the noise and smells of the cities, particularly the heavy coal smoke, and as hard as it would make it to hunt, he'd accepted that the cities were probably a better choice for him now. That was why he was heading for the coast. He covered over fifty kilometres that night before he had to stop to find a cave to hole up in through the day.

Bilal also knew that he would have to blend in in the cities, so he'd need to change his appearance somewhat. He had gold enough, as he'd collected money from the bodies and belongings of those who'd attacked him, or the robbers that he'd taken care of after they'd killed their innocent victims, but he had to start changing his look. He pulled scissors, comb and mirror from his bundle, and while he was holed up in his den for the day, he started by trimming his hair and beard enough to make them acceptable among civilised people. He snorted as he thought that the Sultan who'd prohibited him from wearing a beard was centuries dead now.

He'd also found something he hoped could provide a more acceptable solution than wrapping cloth over his eyes to let him bear the daylight, two sets of goggles that had been in the belongings of one of those robbers' victims should serve for this.

It took him two more nights to reach the nearest sizable port, Rotterdam. There he ordered some decent clothes, shoes and hats to be made up, engaged glass workers to replace the clear glass in the goggles with dark glass and had a walking umbrella made up which concealed a full length triangular small sword blade with a sharpened edge (he'd gotten the idea from sword sticks he'd seen travellers using). As he had to stay in the town for a few days while these were being made up, he took a room in a lodging house, staying in his room most of the day with the blinds drawn. While he was there, he also bought a voluminous carpet bag to replace his bundle, and such other sundries as he expected to need.

He was pleased with the way the clothes, shoes, hats, goggles and umbrella came out, and booked his passage across the channel to England. He would have rather gone to the Americas, but knew that there was no way he could make that voyage without feeding, so England would have to be enough, for now anyway.

The dapper young bearded gentleman who boarded the boat to England, umbrella in one hand, carpet bag in the other, wearing goggles with dark lenses, was William (Bill) Schaffer of Sheffield (according to the papers he carried). Little trace remained of Bilal, the Sultan's Janissary from four hundred odd years earlier, other than the soldier's queue that he wore his hair in. It was fortunate that Bilal had started out as a boy from Bulgaria, as with his blonde hair, skin and features he could pass for English well enough, as could his accent.

A large part of what he'd listened to as he sat on the edge of the towns at night was the language and news of people from other lands. He'd acquired memories from the creature who afflicted him with this, and these memories had included the knowledge of many languages. He'd been updating those languages in his head by listening to people talking, and practising speaking while he was holed up in his den when the sun was up. As a result, he could speak English with only a trace of a foreign accent, and most seemed to accept his explanation that this was because he'd been away, living on the Continent for some years now.

Even on the docks of London, Bill was choking on the heavy pall of coal smoke that hung over the city, and the cacophony of noise was overwhelming, as it was too much for him to filter out. He knew that there was no way that he could stay here, not unless he could find something workable, out on the edge of the city. Desperate for a solution, he decided to try to find lodging opportunities on the edges of London, hoping that the air may be clean enough for him to bear out there. If so, that may also give him the opportunity to slip out of the city to hunt when he needed to.

A few enquiries gave him the necessary directions to 'one of the nicer parts out there, more suitable for a gentleman like yourself', Waltham Forest, and Bill caught the train out there. Once in Waltham Forest, he sniffed the air, and was pleasantly surprised to find that it was relatively fresh, and what's more, he could smell deer, and more, in the woods nearby.

Further enquiries once he arrived led him to a respectable but unprepossessing house owned by an older lady, Mrs Roper, who was taking in boarders, but she was terribly apologetic that the only rooms she had were downstairs, and the light wasn't good down there.

Bill gave a little laugh and tapped his goggles. "With my eyes, Missus Roper, I hardly think that will be a problem."

She laughed nervously at that, saying "No, I suppose not Mister Schaffer." as she led him downstairs.

The rooms were perfect for him, as they were a rather more comfortable and modern version of the dens he'd been living in for the past four hundred odd years, he could easily control the light with curtains and what was more, they had their own external door so he could come and go at night without Mrs Roper or others' knowledge. He nodded to himself. "This will do me nicely Missus Roper, I'll take it."

With naught but the contents of his carpet bag to unpack, it didn't take Bill long to settle in and turn his rooms into a civilised cave, carefully freeing up the outer door so that he could leave quietly when he wished. That done, he settled down to have a nap, as he planned to go prowling that night.

Once night had fallen, Bill rose and slipped out the door, eager to explore this new world that he'd come to. He'd confirmed the train timetables when he came here, and knew that there were sufficient night trains to take him down into London for a few hours, if not more, and bring him back again, and if there were any problems with the trains, he could easily do the fourteen miles on foot before dawn.

The coal smoke was little better in the heart of London at night than it had been during the day, but at least the noise was at a more manageable level for him. Some people steered clear of him, obviously believing he had consumption from the way he was coughing at the coal smoke, but by and large, he was being treated like any other toff on the streets of Soho. People tried to sell him things or asked for money, and the cleaner street whores tried to entice him.

That first night established two standards for Bill's existence in London, the first being that he spent quite a bit of time chatting with the street girls, many of whom became his friends over time (Bill was never a paying customer, nor he would he accept a free hump, but they loved chatting with young Mr Schaffer, he was always the gentleman, and never treating them like dirt as most did). This was to lead him into a dire situation in later years. The other came about when he heard a woman pleading for mercy in a back alley.

Bill excused himself from his discussion, promising to return, and quickly headed for the alley that he'd heard the voice coming from. Once in the dark alley, he could clearly see a well dressed young woman struggling with two rough looking men. One was holding her from behind while the other was groping at her breasts, and both men were laughing.

All three of them looked at him when he said "I think you should let the young lady go, and go about your business."

The men looked at each other, and the one holding the woman threw her down roughly as they charged at him together. Bill released the blade from his umbrella, intending to finish this quickly by running the both of them through, but that hunger came over him as he did so.

He flashed a look at the woman, but she was facing away and dazed from being thrown down. With that, he skewered the one who'd been holding her through the shoulder with the sword blade as he bit into the other's neck. He discovered as he was sucking the life energy from him that he, too, acquired the memories of the victim as he was sucking everything else out of them. This was something he hadn't really noted with the animals that he'd been feeding on, and something he'd rather not do as he saw this one's memories flashing before his eyes. When he'd drained him, he dropped his limp body and turned on the other one, ripping the blade from his shoulder as he did so, and bit into his neck, sucking the life force from him as he struggled.

With the two men drained, he quickly checked that the woman was still unable to see anything. He then slashed their throats, cutting through the bite marks enough to conceal their nature and wiped the blade clean on their clothes before re-sheathing it in the umbrella. Bill went through their pockets, collecting any money and valuables, and shoved their bodies behind some crates before going to help the woman up.

"Miss? Miss, you're safe, they've run off. Are you alight?"

As he asked this, he checked over her, but aside from the bodice and sleeve of her dress being torn, there were no outward signs of harm. Of course being grabbed, dragged back in here and manhandled like that must have terrified her and left her off balance.

The young woman put her hand to her head, blushing as she looked down to see her bodice torn open and her chemise showing, so she was trying to hold her bodice closed as she responded. "Thank you sir, yes, yes, I believe that I am alright."

"Did they hurt you?"

"Not too much, no, thank you sir."

"Well thank heaven for small mercies, now I think we should get you safely home as quickly as possible, are you able to walk?"

"Yes, yes please sir, I, I think so." She took a step forward, but was so unsteady on her feet that he offered her his arm to support her, which she grabbed and hung onto as though her life depended on it.

He led her out of the alley and flagged down a Hansom cab, handing her up into it. As soon as he joined her in the cab, she grabbed his arm again, hanging on tightly.

At the cabbie's 'Where to guv?' Bill tried to get the address from the young woman, but it was difficult getting through to her, as the shock of what had happened had settled in and she was weeping uncontrollably.

It eventually registered when he squeezed her hand, gently saying "Miss, Miss, we need to know where to take you to, where do you live?" and she gathered her wits enough to quietly tell him the address. He repeated it to the cabbie and with that they were in their way.

When they arrived, Bill paid the fare, but asked the driver to wait as he assisted her out of the cab and up to the door. No sooner had he rung the bell than the door swung open.

The doorman's face lit up at the sight of the young woman. "Miss Cecilia is back!" he cried.

At that, a crowd of excited people descended upon them, anxious to determine whether 'Miss Cecilia' was alright, one of whom turned out to be the young man who she'd been with when she was taken by the two men.

They insisted that Bill come in as they determined what happened, and as Cecilia told her story, Bill became angrier by the minute.

"Well, we went to the theatre with our friends, as you know, and afterwards Freddie thought it would be a lark to go down to Soho, but the others didn't think much of the idea, so it was only the two of us who went."

"Those men came up to us and demanded money from us, but when Freddie told them to leave us alone, they hit him and dragged me off to that alley where Mister..."

She turned to Bill. "I'm so sorry sir, you saved me from, well, I don't want to think what you saved me from, and I haven't even asked your name, or thanked you properly yet."

Bill smiled kindly at her. "It was nothing Miss. I merely thought that it sounded as though someone was in trouble and went to investigate, and like most bullies, they cut and ran when they were faced with someone more their size." At that, his face changed as he turned on the young man.

"Which brings us to a very important question, where were you when this (waving to indicate the state of Cecilia's dress) was being done to the young lady?"

Cecilia's family was also very interested in the answer to that question, now that they'd heard what had happened to her, so they all turned to look at Freddie. He drew himself up and haughtily said, "I ran to get the police, of course!"

There was silence in the foyer at that, until Bill spoke in a chill voice. "So after taking her alone into a dangerous part of town at night, when she was grabbed and dragged off into an alley by two men, you ran away?"

"No! I was getting the police. That was the right thing to do!"

Bill raised his voice for the first time since he arrived as he spat out. "There's not one thing that you've done tonight that was right, boy. You disgust me!"

"Just who do you think you're talking to? I doubt that you are even a proper gentleman sir!"

If Freddie had any sense, he would have feared the look that Bill skewered him with as he spoke, but he didn't.

"I'm talking to the pathetic coward who took a young lady, alone, into a dangerous part of town at night in some stupid attempt to make himself appear dashing. Who when confronted with the reality of the place, was prepared to allow his companion to be raped rather than stand up to those men, and *then* left and ran back here instead of even looking for her! And if *you* are what is supposed to be a proper gentleman, *boy*, I will gladly concede your point on that!"

Freddie rushed at Bill at that, enraged, with his fists flailing madly. The measure of Bill's own rage was the fact that, while he did no more than slap him, the blow was enough to drive him into the floor, barely conscious and surely broken. As one, the family turned their backs on the pathetic figure on the floor as if it were beneath notice.

With that, Bill bowed to Cecilia, saying, "I am truly happy that you're home, safe Miss, but I really must be going."

She ran forward in tears to embrace him, whispering, "Thank you!"

Before he could leave, he had to also accept the tearful thanks of both her parents.

As he exited the house, he was pleased to see that the cabbie had indeed waited, but he'd only just settled into the cab and told the cabbie to take him back to Soho where he'd picked them up, when the front door was flung open for Cecilia's father to toss Freddie bodily down the front steps. As Freddie lay on the footpath, groaning, he shouted, "If you ever come near my daughter again, I'll give you a thrashing like you've never had before, coward!" slamming the door as he finished.

The cabbie laughed as he flicked the reins, but as they headed back to Soho he asked, "Forgive me for being bold sir, but was that toff the reason the young lady was in the state she was?"

Bill spat out "Yes!", but he had to smile and nod when he heard the cabbie mutter, "Wish I'd run over him now!"

Back in Soho, he paid the fare, plus a little extra for waiting as he'd asked, and went back to apologise to the girl he'd been talking to when he heard Cecilia. When he reached her though, she threw her arms around his neck and kissed him, but before he could draw back she started whispering urgently in his ear.

"You have to get out of here! Someone found the bodies of those two bastards and enough folk have talked to the police that they're looking for someone who looks like you! They'll forget about this in a day or so, none will miss bastards like that, but for now you have to go!"

Bill kissed her on the cheek, whispering "Thank you!" in her ear and pressing a few notes into her hand. When she tried to give them back he closed her hand over them and smiled, moving like a ghost off to the station.

On the train back to Chingford, Bill considered the events of the evening, and realised that those two thugs had shown him a way forward. He could protect others from those who preyed on them, while at the same time he could feed without exposing himself. After all, as he'd reasoned at the time, if he was going to kill these scum anyway, why not make use of them and feed? Emptying their pockets after he'd killed them would also provide him with the income he needed to pay his bills.

That night provided the structure for Bill's life for the next ten years or so. Every two or three nights at least (usually more), Bill would slip out of his rooms and catch the train down into London. He moved about a bit, following the majority of his friends as they were told to work other areas, but the pattern was the same. He'd talk to his friends, the working girls and others, give them a little money to help cover their bills, and if he heard the sounds of mayhem, he'd go off and deal with it.

All in all, this life worked for Bill, as he had companionship and friendship. (The girls couldn't understand why he'd let none of them, even the prettiest, do anything for him to repay him. They didn't really believe what he said about being worried that he might get carried away and hurt them, not him, but they could see the truth in his eyes when he told them that he valued their friendship more. They valued his friendship too, as his gift of happiness and laughter did much to offset the rest of their world) He also managed to protect people from those who would prey on them by removing those predators. In doing this, he addressed his need to feed and made himself a pretty penny as he emptied their pockets once he'd drained them, so it was good for him as well as everyone else, except the predators.

This all changed when he moved into the Whitechapel area in the second half of eighty eight, following his friends. The feel of the place was off, and the reason became clear as the girls started getting killed. First it was Martha. Her death angered him, all the more-so because he couldn't find her killer, but he didn't realise that it was more than that until Polly was killed about three weeks later, and then Annie just over a week after her.

Bill was frustrated that he couldn't find their killer, and he tried to get the girls to stop working, telling them that it wasn't safe, but they didn't listen, not until both Liz and Kate were killed on the same night three weeks or so after Annie. The girls listened then, and took care, and this freed him to devote more time to the hunt for this killer, but he was getting nowhere!

He kept searching, but it was to no avail until about five weeks after Liz and Kate's deaths, when a carriage passed him in the hours before dawn, and he caught the scent he'd picked up where the girls were killed, along with the scent of old blood. He followed this carriage, and when it stopped at a quiet house in one of the better neighbourhoods, he waited until its occupant had gone inside before he took the driver, seeing enough in his memories to confirm that the killer of his friends, the Whitechapel killer, was inside.

He quietened the horses and then slipped into the house. He made sure that there wasn't anyone else inside and then, finding the man trying to wash the blood off himself, he took him, draining him.

Bill's problems only began here, though, because as he took in this man's memories, he not only saw what he'd done to the girls (and especially Mary, sweet little Mary, for all her faults she was a nice girl, and she certainly didn't deserve *that*), he saw what else this fiend had been. The Queen's secret lover!

He had to get away after that, out of England if he knew what was good for him, so he went through the house, collecting what money and valuables he could find, along with the trophies the killer had been taking from the girls. Bill stopped to think at that point, and trying on the man's clothes, found that they fitted him well enough, so he packed a suitable wardrobe for an extended trip into the man's trunks, carrying these out to the carriage as well.

He cut up the bodies of both the man and his driver, bundling them up to contain the blood before he cleaned the house quickly, locked it up and left. His first stop was the Thames, and luckily it was ebb tide. That meant that as he tossed in the men's body parts and the trophies that the killer had taken, they were all washed out to sea, along with the apron the killer used. The instruments and jars he'd used didn't float, but Bill's anger ensured that they were cast far out into the river before they sank.

His next stop was Mrs. Roper's house, where he collected his things and left a note with six months' extra rent and departed, locking the external door behind him. He sold the carriage and horses to one who dealt in such things, and then hailed a Hackney coach to take him and the trunks to the offices of the new airship company to book immediate passage to America, as Albert Drake.

The Queen would never know why her lover left her and ran away to America, and Bill, no, Albert, ardently hoped that she didn't know about the other side of her lover, for the sake of England.

Neale Green writes in a number of styles, steampunk (perhaps other punks as well, if the urge arises), sci- fi, adventure, horror, fantasy, more often than not a mix of more than one and with a dash of comedy and romance thrown in for flavour. He hails from Sydney, Australia, and is trying to avoid going back into the world of corporate and government security.

You may find more at: http://punkfiction.weebly.com/the-forum/category/neale-green

THE COMPLICATIONS OF AVERY VANE

BRYCE RAFFLE

Avery Vane, Avery Vane
Wicked, twisted, and insane
Killed his wife and ate her brain
Then killed his son and did the same

AVERY VANE WAS SEATED COMFORTABLY on the divan, puffing white rings of smoke from his cigarette, when the knock came at the door. He dashed out the butt of his smoke, and wiping his hands on his handkerchief, got out of his seat. He moved over to the door, and waited there for his butler to announce who was calling. To his surprise, it was not his butler that he met in the den, but the doctor.

Avery visibly flinched and stumbled away from his uninvited guest. Avery's butler trailed behind the doctor, spewing apologies. "I'm sorry, sir. I'm afraid he rather insisted."

Avery's hands tightened into fists, barely suppressed rage threatening to bubble and spill over. The doctor carried with him a sea of uncomfortable memories. A wave of them flooded Avery's mind, memories he'd tried desperately to rid himself of. The doctor was a reminder of wicked deeds, of the monster within Avery that threatened to claw its way to the surface and take over once more.

Avery was a different man now. He was reformed. The monster was under control, and the doctor was nothing more than a reminder of the man he'd once been. It bothered him that the man had something to hold over him, that he owed him anything. Avery should have dealt with this problem long ago. He was tired of letting the doctor push him around.

"That's fine, Mr. Duncan, I'll see the doctor in the den. If you could start a fire, it would be much appreciated. I felt a cold breeze sweep into the room when the door opened." He probably sounded more at ease than he felt. The cigarette might have helped with that. He turned to his uninvited guest, determined to be civil, even if it killed him. "To what do I owe the pleasure, Dr. Jekyll?"

"Pleasure?" Dr. Jekyll repeated. "I must say, you don't appear pleased to see me."

The doctor, according to habit, wore a black leather mask, in the old-fashioned style of plague doctors. Mr. Vane had yet to ascertain the reason for the strange accoutrement, but frankly, he found the mask unsettling. Not once had he seen the doctor's face. The doctor's voice was muffled, almost to the point of being incomprehensible. Avery had once noticed a small vent on the underside of the mask, through which he could hear the doctor's ragged breath.

"This is my apprentice," he said.

Avery blinked. Apprentice?

He hadn't noticed the young boy, who now stepped out from behind the doctor. The boy, although unmasked, was equally frightening to look at. His skin was so pale it was practically translucent. His hair was white. Not blonde, but white, as stark as snow. His eyes were a soft pink, his lashes as pale as his hair. Avery had never seen anyone like him, in all his years.

"How do you do?" he managed.

He hoped he sounded polite. It wasn't like Avery to stare. He'd been raised according to a strict set of manners. His mother would have rapped his knuckles with an ash branch for how he was staring at the little albino.

It wasn't just the boy's pale complexion that disturbed Avery. There was something in his expression. Something unsettling. Perhaps it was just the boy's pink eyes that prejudiced Vane against the unfortunate youth, but Avery imagined he saw hatred in those eyes. Cold, calculating hatred.

Avery forced a smile. He realized that the doctor had not yet answered his question. Sitting back down on the divan, he fished out another cigarette and lit it nervously. He gestured to the empty chairs.

"Can I offer you anything, doctor? Tea? Perhaps something stronger?"

"We won't be staying long," the doctor answered.

Neither he, nor the boy, had taken a seat. Instead, they stood at the threshold of the den. Strangely, Avery felt cornered, like a caged animal. It was ridiculous of him to be so intimidated by the old doctor and the young boy who trailed behind him. Surely if they wanted to hurt him, he could fight them off. The boy looked as frail as a ghost, and he had always assumed that the doctor was well past his prime. Avery, meanwhile, was in his twenties, tall, and athletic. If need be, he could call for help, and a dozen servants would be with him in a minute. He was dangerous. Even years after what had happened, people feared him, rumors continued to circulate around him. Women crossed the street when passing his house and grown men avoided looking in his eyes when they saw him about town.

He was Avery Goddamn Vane. Children sang rhymes about him. They whispered his name into the mirror on dares, fearing he would suddenly manifest behind them.

Avery Vane, Avery Vane,

Wicked, twisted, and insane.

And yet…

"What do you want?" he sneered.

"Come with us," the doctor replied. "We have something to discuss."

"Whatever it is, we can discuss it here," said Avery. He was disappointed with himself. He'd meant to sound forceful, determined. Instead, his voice trembled and cracked.

"This will all go much more smoothly if you do as I say, Mr. Vane."

"No," he said again. His voice was softer this time, barely more than a whisper. His lips trembled. He cursed himself for being so weak.

"Mr. Vane, it is really not my style to adopt such an unsavory practice as blackmail, but I'm afraid I really must insist that you come with me at once. Otherwise..."

The doctor didn't need to finish that sentence. Avery knew exactly what the doctor held over him. If his secret got out, Avery would be ruined. Sure, there were rumors, but the doctor had more than that. He had proof. He wouldn't just be ruined—he'd be utterly destroyed.

The way Avery saw it, he had only two options. He could go along with the doctor. Or he could put a bullet in the doctor's chest. He'd have to kill the child too. He didn't like the idea of killing another child, especially now that he was reformed. But he was tired of letting the doctor intimidate him. Wasn't it time to let the monster out?

He drew his pistol. He wished he could see the look on the doctor's face. The sudden transition from arrogance to fear. The doctor raised his arms as if to plead for his life, and took a step back. Avery readied the pistol, aimed it at the doctor's chest.

"Hyde," said the doctor.

Avery blinked. What?

Then he felt an enormous hand engulfing his skull. He felt himself being whirled around like a rag doll. The pistol fell to the floor with a clatter, and Avery found himself face to face with Death.

The man—if he was a man at all—wore a weathered black plague mask, like the doctor's, only much larger. He was dressed in a black cowl. He was also the biggest man Avery had seen in his life. Giant bastard must have come in through the back door. Without a word, he lifted Avery off his feet with one hand, by his hair. Avery felt strands of hair rip from his scalp. He screamed.

Then, with what seemed like no effort at all, the giant flung Avery across the room. He crashed into the settee, landed hard on the floor, and lay there. Unable to move, he stared at the ceiling.

No one had come to his rescue. Avery began to wonder if his servants were even still alive.

"Well done, Mr. Hyde," said the doctor.

The albino child hunched over Avery. His pale white face was all Avery could see.

"Help me," he pleaded. Surely he'd only imagined the hatred in the boy's eyes. He was just a child, after all. "Please. Run and call for help."

The boy smiled. For a moment, Avery thought that the boy was going to do as he asked. Then the boy opened his mouth and let a big ball of spit spill out onto Avery's forehead. Avery groaned.

The boy smiled at his handiwork. Then he began to kick Avery. He wasn't terribly strong, but Avery couldn't move at all. His ribs had probably been broken in the fall, and each kick made him wince with pain. Eventually, he lost consciousness.

Avery Vane awoke with a sudden fluttering of his eyelids. The harsh light made him squint. As his eyes began to adjust, he discovered that the room was actually dimly lit by a single oil lamp, which had been thrust into his face. He turned away from the harshness of the light, and took a look around the room.

It was a laboratory. This, he could surmise from the test tubes, beakers, and other scientific equipment that lined the shelves, and from the preparations on the tables. Dissections of animals, as well as human organs, were preserved in jars of formaldehyde.

"So glad you're awake," said the doctor, still with his mask on. "My apologies. Mr. Hyde often forgets his own strength."

The giant grunted and shuffled awkwardly on his feet. It might actually have been a genuine apology. Not that Avery could say the same for the doctor's feigned civility.

The doctor set the oil lamp on the table, giving Avery the chance to look at him without staring directly into the harsh light. He noticed that the albino was no longer with them.

"So," the doctor continued. "I regret Mr Hyde's roughness, Mr. Vane, but I do hope that it has given you an appreciation for how serious I am about the boy's welfare."

"The boy?" Avery repeated. "What does this have to do with him?"

"Mr. Vane, I need not remind you—and don't believe for a moment that I'm merely pandering to your ego—that you are by far the best clockmaker in the country. I might even go so far as to say you are the best in the world."

"Your point, Dr. Jekyll?" Avery asked, impatiently.

Pandering to his ego, indeed! Avery snorted with distaste. He looked straight into the doctor's face. It was unnerving that he couldn't see the man's eyes, as they were hidden behind the mask's tinted lenses. Nor could he recognize his voice, as it was distorted by the mask, which meant that there was no way of determining who the doctor really was. Jekyll was almost certainly an alias, borrowed from Robert Louis Stevenson's story. Avery read the penny dreadfuls.

"My point, Mr. Vane, is that I've been taking on the responsibility of educating the boy. He's very bright, you see, and very keen, and his father wants to provide him with the very best opportunities. I have an obligation which requires me to be away for a couple of months—"

"No," Avery said. He could see perfectly well where this was going.

"He'll be an excellent student," the doctor continued, heedless of the interruption, "although he bores easily. Did you know, I left for several months not too long ago; I arranged for young Jack to sit in at the university. He grew so bored he decided to open his own surgical practice, and when I returned from my business, I learned that Jack had been cutting classes every day and operating a rather successful business as a surgeon. He wore a mask, like mine, so that no one would realize he was only thirteen, but his expertise as a surgeon is quite remarkable. Not just for a boy his age, but for any surgeon. I'm sure he'll be quick to pick up the fine art of clockmaking, especially with you to—"

"No," Avery said again.

"No?" the doctor repeated. He stood over Avery, who was seated on the floor, with his back against the wall. The effect was that the doctor seemed to tower over him. "Do you not see the position you're in, Mr. Vane? Did you not see how easy it was for me and my associate to invite ourselves into your home?"

Avery refused to be intimidated. He spat. A great gob of spit landed square on the doctor's right lens. Calmly, almost as if nothing out of the ordinary had happened, the doctor withdrew a handkerchief. He wiped the spit from his lens.

"Need I remind you about that unfortunate bit of bad business I helped you with a year ago? A little thing like that can come back to bite you. It was only lucky that you had such a dear friend as me to help you out. You might want to consider how you treat such friends."

"Friends? You're a tyrant. A bully. We're not friends, Doctor. Do what you must. Tell the police if you must, but I won't work for you."

"Come now, be reasonable. Do you need to be reminded of what you did, Vane?"

"I'm well aware of what I did. There isn't a day that goes by that it doesn't haunt me."

"And you'll really let me tell the police?" asked Dr. Jekyll.

"I won't let you intimidate me."

"There is one other thing," said the doctor. "If blackmail doesn't frighten you, if the threat of violence doesn't intimidate you, there is still one more thing."

"What?"

"Your disease," Jekyll said. His words oozed out of his mouth, slimy and foul.

Avery felt his heart stop, like a train that had run out of coal. Dead on its tracks. "What about it?"

"What would happen to you if your access to your medicine was suddenly cut off?" asked the doctor.

A lump formed in Avery's throat. He tried to swallow, but his mouth was dry as ash.

"I keep a personal supply in a number of locations, known only to me," Avery said. "Just in case."

The doctor barked out a single, cold laugh, a harsh and metallic sound as it was filtered through the mask's tubes and vents.

"Very enterprising of you, Mr. Vane. But let's suppose that somebody discovered the locations of your secret supplies. What would become of you then?"

Avery swallowed. He stared back at the doctor, his jaw set.

Jekyll stood. He beckoned to Mr. Hyde, and with the giant at his side, he headed into the corner of the room. A big steel cage stood there, atop a wheeled cart. Together, Jekyll and Hyde wheeled the cart into the center of the room. It was clear that Hyde was doing most of the work. As the cart drew closer, Avery began to make out what was inside the cage.

"I'll tell you what would become of you," said the doctor. "First, your skin would begin to die. It would peel off in strips and flake away like it does after a sunburn. Then you would begin to rot. Then, finally, when your body has all but died, your mind would be surrendered to the disease. An insatiable hunger would come over you. The urge to hunt for prey, to kill, and to eat. I mentioned at your home, I had something to show you."

He gestured to the cage. It held a monster within its bars. It was a monster that Avery recognized. This thing was human once, its skin torn and peeling, its putrid flesh grey with rot, its eyes emotionless and predatory. It snarled, baring yellow teeth and a blackened tongue. It banged its maggot-ridden hands against the iron bars of its cage. There was no indication of intelligence in its eyes, just raw aggression and hunger. This was the monster within Avery. This was what would become of him if Jekyll were to cut off his supply of medication.

"Can't you do anything to help it?" he asked, "Like you helped me?"

"Unfortunately, no. The disease is too far gone. This poor wretch is beyond saving. And if you were to stop taking your medicine for too long..." The doctor trailed off, letting the thought sink in. At a certain point, even his medication wouldn't be enough to keep Avery's monster at bay. He needed regular doses of his medicine just to remain human.

At last, Avery let out a breath of air through his nostrils, a sigh of distress. He could see no way out of this.

"What, specifically, do you want me to teach this boy of yours?"

The doctor didn't relish in his victory. He answered calmly as ever, as if he'd been entirely confident of the outcome of the conversation. "I've prepared an itinerary. So long as you follow it, and the boy comes to no harm while I'm away, I will ensure that your medicine continues to arrive on schedule," he said. "Oh, and there's one more thing."

"Which is?"

"Should his father come to inquire after his well being, you are to telegraph me straight-away. Tell the father that I've gone away on urgent business, and that I'll be back shortly. Do not, under any circumstances, allow the father to learn that I am away long-term, or that you've been instructing the boy."

It was strange. For all the doctor's bravado, his intimidation, his posturing, his threats—if Avery didn't know better, he would have guessed that Dr. Jekyll was afraid. It was impossible to say for certain. He could hardly judge by the man's face, nor even by the cadence of his voice, but there was a tightness in the way he held his posture, when he spoke of the boy's father.

Avery nodded, and the tension seemed to melt away.

"Good," said the doctor. "Very good. I'll have Mr. Hyde return you to your home. I hope you don't mind wearing a blindfold. I'd prefer to keep my whereabouts a private matter, for now. You understand, don't you?"

Again, Avery nodded.

"Good," said the doctor.

As it turned out, Avery's ribs were not broken, although they were bruised badly enough that he winced in pain whenever he stooped over or stood up too quickly. His household staff hadn't been murdered, as he'd feared. They'd been rendered unconscious by the doctor's brutish accomplice, but they had recovered well enough. Soon, the doctor's visit was little more than a bad memory, and Avery was back to his usual routine, with one singular exception. Much as he resented the doctor for burdening him with the responsibility of tutoring Jack, he could not fault the boy.

In fact, his young apprentice was an admirable student, with a tireless work ethic and the keen interest that only a child can have. He had spat on Avery's face, but he had since apologized, and the act had been encouraged by Dr. Jekyll. Once away from the doctor's influence, the boy's behavior was considerably different.

He was quiet, patient, and intelligent. Avery soon came to feel that he had misjudged Jack. That cruel look he thought he'd seen in Jack's eyes was imagined, more likely a result of Avery's prejudice against the boy's strange looks than anything else.

Jack was an avid reader, as Avery came to find out. He devoured Avery's texts on clockmaking, but on more than one occasion, he had caught the boy reading penny dreadfuls. The Mysteries of London was his favorite—and he enjoyed pretending that he was Anthony Tidkins, the grave-robber from the stories. The Resurrection Man.

In his spare time, Jack began to apply Avery's lessons and those gleaned from the pages of his books to tinkering with little gadgets and inventions of his own devising. Avery saw no harm in letting him borrow scraps from his pile to devote to these side projects. Jack's surgical knowledge, and his small, steady hands, proved useful in clockmaking, and Avery felt certain that given enough time, Jack would eventually surpass even him.

He showed him how to make a simple pocket watch, and Jack replicated it perfectly. He presented Jack with a broken clock and asked him to repair it. It was ticking away within half an hour.

After a while, Avery actually came to enjoy having the boy around, even if he was only there because of the doctor's threats. In a way, Jack reminded Avery of the son he'd once had. He often caught himself staring at Jack, wondering what his son would be like now, if he were still alive. He would have been about Jack's age.

As the days turned to weeks and the weeks to months, the doctor's return loomed ominously on the calendar. Avery was saddened to think that he would lose his student.

Eventually, he decided to broach the subject with Jack. "Perhaps when the doctor returns, you could continue to study with me," he said, "If you like."

Avery wasn't sure what he'd been expecting. Gratitude, perhaps? Eagerness? Instead, he received a cold look, the same deadpan stare that he'd first seen upon meeting Jack. He hadn't imagined it, after all.

"I see little need for that," Jack replied. "I'm beginning to feel I've already learned everything you can possibly teach me."

Avery clenched his fist, his hand shaking violently. He reminded himself that Jack was just a boy, and that he'd had a rather queer upbringing. Perhaps with the right mentor, Jack could still learn to refine his behavior, his manners.

"I find that clockmaking has a great deal in common with surgery, but it is much simpler, by comparison. After all, what are human beings if not incredibly complicated machines?" Jack continued. "Having mastered surgery, clockmaking seems beneath my skill. Any child could do it."

Avery snorted. "You are a child," he reminded Jack.

He would not stand here and have his trade so crudely insulted. Any hint of the patient, passionate boy Avery had come to know and love was gone, replaced with the cruel, arrogant brat who'd spat on his face. There was a duality in Jack, a duality Avery had once seen in himself when the disease had taken hold of him. Avery was not the man he'd once been—there was a monster within him, just beneath the surface. So long as he took his medicine, he could keep the monster at bay. And Jack was not the same boy who'd spat on his face and who stood before him now. This version of Jack was someone different, a second personality that lay dormant within him. This was Jack's monster.

All this time that Avery had been teaching Jack the art of clockmaking, the other Jack had been there, somewhere distant in the dark recesses of Jack's mind. It wasn't sickness that brought him forth, at least not a physical sickness. Perhaps a mental illness, or perhaps it was just that duality that exists in all men.

Avery took a deep breath. "You overestimate your own skill as a clockmaker," he said, "And you underestimate the complexity of clocks. Your analogy is apt; people are indeed like complicated machines, but the tools used in clockmaking are vastly different from those used by a surgeon. We use calipers and die plates, rivet pliers, and turns, where surgeons use scalpels, bone saws, and forceps. We work with metal, where surgeons deal in flesh. What makes a clock tick is not the same as what makes a man tick."

Jack raised an eyebrow. At least, Avery had his attention.

"Do you know what it's called when a timepiece includes a feature that goes beyond simply displaying hours and minutes?"

"Complications," he answered.

Avery was hardly surprised that Jack already knew the answer. He would have read a dozen books on the subject by now.

"So far, I've only taught you simple movements. Perhaps that was my mistake. I'm not accustomed to having a student. No wonder you're beginning to tire of horology. Why don't we try something with complications?"

Jack smiled, and nodded enthusiastically. The other Jack was gone again. Like a leech sucking the bad blood out of an infected wound, it was boredom that drew out the other Jack. The doctor had warned him that Jack was easily susceptible to boredom. Only now did Avery grasp what that meant.

"It is my firm belief that clocks can be just as complicated as people, depending on the skill of the clockmaker," Avery told him. "If man is made by god, and machine is made by man, suppose you could build a machine as complex as man. What would that make you?"

"God," Jack answered.

Avery nodded. "Now, tell me. Are you still bored?"

Bryce Raffle writes steampunk, horror, and fantasy. He worked as a writer on Ironclad Games' *Sins of a Dark Age*, and is currently working on his debut novel, *Dead London*. He lives in beautiful Vancouver, Canada, where he works as a sound designer for video games and films.

Twitter @bryceraffle
Facebook.com/bryceraffle
Website: www.bryceraffle.com

HARK! HARK!

N.O.A. RAWLE

Hark! Hark!
The dogs will bark
When the beggars have come to town
Races in rags,
split like jags;
Their queen in a velvet gown.

Excerpt from the Anapa Scripts.

CAPTAIN ODAN MACKENZIE MANEUVERED the *Lady Lana,* stratospheric vacuum tanker, carefully watching that the rear docking mast didn't pierce the quartet of ballonets. The airship stretched a full fifty yards longer than the space available for safety measures to be applicable and the other vessels in the vicinity made precision essential.

The *Lady Lana* was a sight to behold. The only stratospheric tanker; she had drawn quite a crowd. Once secured, Mackenzie chanced a proud glance at the observatory, whose windows were now lined with spectators, the select few who could afford this refuge from the decay of Gaskell City. However, it was not the melee which drew his gaze, but a dark female silhouette in the windows of the suite on the upper trajectory. As if registering his attention, she sank back into the shadows. Mackenzie shivered and pulled his fur rimmed hood further forward over his leather helmet, the winged disc, the *Lady Lana*'s emblem, glinting in the weak light.

"A-hoy- there!" the thick accent of the Queen's envoy reached him in fits and starts carried away by the bitter wind that whipped round the Gods' Dock landing platform as Captain Mackenzie ordered his First Mate Mr. Grazenby and the crew to be on standby and double-check the moorings.

"How nice to see you again." Barnet Eidenbury took Mackenzie's proffered hand in his thickly gloved one and ushered the captain inside - and not a moment too soon - as the flurries of snow, precursors of the coming storm, were beginning to fall.

"You too Barnet, old friend. I just wish the circumstances were better," said the captain as he shrugged off his overcoat and handed his helmet and goggles to the waiting valet.

The Gods' Dock was Acantina's highest landing mast, situated near the peak of Mount Oliana. The bar there was affectionately known as the Den, by the aviators and adventurers who frequented the northern regions. The familial warmth and friendly, neutral ground it provided, regardless of the wars waged elsewhere, was a true port in any storm. Mackenzie smiled, a fire danced in the grate and the chairs closest to it were already occupied, a thrum of chatter filled the air along with an aroma of tea and the spiced alcohol that was the speciality of the region. Taking a small table in an alcove to the left of the fireplace, near one of the picture windows, though the panoramic view of the plain of Acantina from the peak of Mount Oliana was obscured. The flurry of flakes that brushed the glass gave the impression they were sitting in the middle of a snow cloud.

Odan Mackenzie took a deep breath but the welcome easing of his muscles did not follow. He smoothed his red beard and moustache in the reflection before turning to the envoy. "How is the situation?"

"Since you've been away harvesting, guerrilla troops have used the drought as an excuse to up their attacks from beyond the northern peaks and refugees have flooded the city fit to bursting. Supplies are dwindling and I do not foresee easy resolution."

"That is not good news, my friend. But how can I be expected to help? The *Lady Lana* is not a battleship and would be too easy a target to run supplies despite her considerable size. Short of doubling ozone harvesting expeditions, which are already putting my crew under enormous strain, I don't see what I can do."

Eidenbury templed his fingers, as if contemplating what he was going to say. Mackenzie knew this look and it meant trouble.

"What crazy scheme do you have up your sleeve?"

"What I am about to ask of you could be the making or the breaking of Acantina, do you understand?"

"Of course. You know where my allegiance lies."

"If I were to tell you that Queen Veriam had a daughter, illegitimate, but heir to the throne, where would you stand then?"

"You are not serious?"

"Very much so. We have to get her into the capital and reinstate the royal line and fast."

"Why did the Queen never make this public? War could have been avoided."

"You will understand and very soon, but you have to swear allegiance to the royal line before I introduce you."

"Is there proof of her lineage?"

"Seeing her will be proof enough — the resemblance is startling — but in answer to your question, yes, there is proof."

"So why all this skullduggery?"

"Do you swear allegiance?"

In all their years serving under the winged disk emblem, Mackenzie had never seen the Eidenbury so anxious nor so excited. Why was this child shrouded in secrecy? Acantina was so unstable that any chance of retaining it would go down well. If the royal line was proven to still exist, the rebel warlords would be guilty of treason.

"I swear." He spoke with a tang of apprehension that he couldn't explain.

"Good." Eidenbury waved the waiter over and whispered something to him that Mackenzie couldn't catch. He stared out at the swirling snow white on grey and watched as it gathered along the sill.

"There are many things the Queen kept secret about her life. For one, her marriage to Lord Beldram was out of convenience, a strategic move—"

"That's common knowledge. She had to do whatever was necessary to keep Acantina secure at the northern borders. Ozone harvesting was too precious to risk over territorial squabbles. If water purification had failed, we'd have died out decades ago."

"How easily the stories are bought." Eidenbury leaned back into the warm leather of the wing-backed chair as he spoke.

"One believes the most logical story one hears; truth is but a perspective on any given event."

"True enough." Eidenbury admitted.

"The story you will hear tonight is far from logical, but it is not mine to tell. I must ask you one more time: Do you swear allegiance?"

Mackenzie replied solemnly, "Of that, you can be assured."

Eidenbury simply nodded and rose from the chair. Mackenzie took his lead and they traversed the length of the Den and out into the deserted hallway. Barnet Eidenbury led him up the wooden stairs and along the silent corridor lit only by the eerie cool light of the swirling snow outside. They stopped at the far end where three steps took them down to an insubstantial wooden door. Eidenbury rapped before opening and leading the captain inside.

Silhouetted against the wild billowing snow in the bay window that formed the bow end of the Gods' Dock was the woman Odan Mackenzie had glimpsed earlier. As she remained motionless, her back to them, Mackenzie stared openly. She was dressed in a long flowing velvet gown of the deepest blue. The fabric draped in deep swathes along with a thick cloak attached by two clasps to her shoulders so it left her back bared and shimmering in the cool light. The cloak was of a fabric he couldn't discern. With her hair dressed in peacock feathers, the princess was better dressed for dinner than staging an attack to reclaim her throne.

"Your Highness." Eidenbury bowed low and long; Mackenzie followed suit in a flustered shuffle. As she turned towards them, his gasp was more audible than he would have wished.

"Please, gentlemen. I do not want sycophants, but leaders."

Eidenbury turned as crimson as his cravat. "Your Highness, may I introduce Captain Odan Mackenzie of the *Lady Lana*. Captain, the Princess Petaxi."

"I saw your craft, she is impressive." Her smile was demure, genuine, and so utterly beguiling. She was the very likeness of her mother except that she was half Avianou.

"Thank you, Your Highness."

"Will it be up to flying me into Gaskell City? I need to get to the palace and reclaim my rightful place." The comment was made without a touch of irony in her voice.

Mackenzie swallowed, already regretting his promise. The woman was clearly mad. Did she not realise there was a war being fought in Acantina – one fought over lineage and purity. How would those whose allegiance to the royal house was because of its pure human lineage be able to assimilate the uniquely human beauty of Queen Veriam and the exotic allure of the Avianou race both personified in the Princess Petaxi?

"Well?"

"Your Highness, the suitability of my ship is unquestionable." Mackenzie fumbled for words, uncertain as to how he should express his fears, "You have anatomical differences that would be hard to address, even if we had the best prostheticians at hand." Direct honesty was clearest.

"I am well aware of my *differences,* but why should that be a problem when I so obviously am the heir?"

She strode into the light. Her dark, almond shaped eyes bore the unmistakable royal characteristics, the long nose and high forehead. However, what had appeared to be her hair dressed so extravagantly was in fact plumage evidence of her Avianou descent. A simple gown was all she wore and the cloak, the majestic cloak of layers of lustrous feathers in jewelled greens and peacock blues, was no garment at all, but wings.

She smiled and gestured the two men towards the couches that were set in the niche all around the bay window. Seating herself elegantly on a long ottoman allowing her wings space to layout behind her, she turned her attention to the table where there was a steaming urn of spiced tea the Den was so famous for.

"I am told it is laced with the finest vodka and spices, embodying all Acantina. It is the epitome of what we are, don't you think? Sugar from the south," she placed a little in each of the porcelain cups, "Vodka from the north and eastern spiced tea. I have taken the liberty of adding Harrakuppa, from the west, to complete the symbolism."

"To Acantina." The princess raised her cup and drank deeply.

Mackenzie smelled the tangy aroma of Harrakuppa, the hallucinogenic wild spice so favoured by the Avianou for their rituals, and knew that he would not be seeing straight before mid morning. He too drained his cup.

Eidenbury looked regretfully into his but did not partake of the spiced liquid.

"I have seen the vision; please exclude me this time - I will watch the door."

The drug took very little time to affect Mackenzie's sensibilities. Soon the princess began to glow before him, her wing feathers like a thousand eyes boring into his soul. She crawled up to him as would an impatient child, her long fingers caressing his cheek, her spiced breath tantalizing his every muscle. Tearing his gaze away, aware of her laughter he let his head loll back on the sill of the window and gazed up towards the snow flurries.

He felt as if he were falling upwards, sucked towards the stratosphere. He glimpsed a snapshot of the *Lady Lana* in all her glory, her hull firmly moored, in his mind's eye, he refocused to Mr. Grazenby, alert on the bridge. Then he sped on, further up, lingering momentarily on the pearlescent sheen of the snow capping the peak of the Mount Oliana, up — straight up — into the chill air beyond. As he soared so, he found he was not alone; by his side was the princess, her dark feathered hair streaming out behind her and her wings spread wide, flying beside him, golden bronze skin shimmering in the sunlight.

"Where are we going?" he asked, his voice sounding shrill and keen under the effects of the Harrakuppa.

"Back to my birth. Had I simply told you, you would never have believed it."

He nodded and let her take his hand in hers. Her long and golden bronze fingers had a subtle luminescence. Now she was in the lead the air rushed past him ruffling his hair chilling his hands. Sensing this, her talon-like fingers closed tighter around his and she hefted him faster and higher until they had reached the plain of the Avianou.

From here, the vastness of the universe spread above, beckoning but as yet unexplored by humankind. Below him the curvature of the earth glowed at first as if molten gold were being poured along its edge until at last the sunlight spilled over the lip and Acantina was illuminated, the clouds scudding below like sheep herded in distant fields. The oceans glittered in the morning light like seas of jewels. The princess beckoned him onwards and the vision was doused in shadow. He looked up, the *Lady Lana* soared above but how was that so without him at her helm?

"Good, you see her too. But she is captained by your predecessor."

"But that's—"

"Impossible? No. You are now witnessing the joint memories of the Avianou. This is a rare privilege, but you must understand what is at stake if the guerrillas gain total control of Acantina and deny the Avianou. Our kinds have been inter-connected for longer than mankind can fathom but, unlike you, we do not forget because we carry the history of our kind in our blood."

Odan Mackenzie watched the *Lady Lana* float serenely upwards towards the more than familiar realms of the stratosphere where he had spent as long as he could remember harvesting Ozone. As a lad he had dreamed of nothing less than becoming a sky captain which his role on the missions more than fulfilled. Few wanted to travel so far because of the risks involved, not only from the extreme cold and thin air, but from the threat posed by the Avianou who begrudgingly shared their supplies of Ozone with humanity.

In the vision, the *Lady Lana* was making no ordinary mission. Aboard was King Ruben, Petaxi's grandfather, and his envoy.

"I know what this is," Mackenzie smiled. He had learned about it in history. "It's when King Ruben forced the hand of the Avianou, making them see sense, and understanding with regard to their position in the greater scheme of Acantina.

"Hold your tongue before you come to regret that you have spoken. You may know what history teaches but there is no better document than living memory."

Mackenzie recoiled at Petaxi's fury. But the next time she spoke it was as if her outburst had never happened.

"We see things as they happened and you too will learn of the fallacies you have been led to believe as history, see,"

As if she had laid out the past on the sky before him, so he now saw the king and his entourage disembark from the *Lady*

Lana and made a grand procession across the largest plain that served as a roost for the Avianou.

They were greeted by a man not so unlike Petaxi although he shared none of her human features. His face was smooth and void of eyes for they were either side of his head, just forward of where a human would have ears. The Avianou had no obvious ears or mouth but three tiny gill-like protrusions in their places, through which they filtered the fine air of space.

"Thank you." King Ruben bowed low to the chief Avianou. "You know my purpose well before I speak of it so I will not waste words. I have come to beg you that we might harvest ozone within your domain so that we may cleanse our water. Our land will die; we have been cursed by—"

"By your own hand! You come wielding utterances of possession when you cannot even protect that which you claim to own!" The Avianou chief's voice reverberated with fury.

He paced away from the King who turned to his envoy for support but before he could respond, the Avianou continued, "Ozone is not mine; I can neither grant permission nor prevent you from harvesting it. Your materialistic ways are as alien to me as you are, and although the purpose for your greed is incomprehensible to us, I know enough to see that it is down to me to ensure that you will never take more than you need. Avianou share the upper-reaches of the atmosphere as a communal space like we share our memories, inherited through generations. We have lived this way for as long as we remember, with no need or desire for possession or innovation, for millennia before mankind even considered the possibility of the heavens being accessible. You perceived us as angels or gods, if we were seen at all. But since mankind has discovered flight, our existence has been threatened. No treaties have stayed off the murderers who wantonly slaughter Avianou for sport and so I know your promises of restraint when it comes to harvesting of ozone are worthless. However, I am forced to recognise that we must coexist if either of our kinds is to survive and that demands a radical solution. To that end, I propose an exchange."

Mackenzie cringed as King Ruben smarted at the accusations, but acknowledged that he must have had very little in the way of control over his subjects with regard to hunting. As for the ozone harvests, he was ashamed to say the assessment was probably true.

"Both our people's lives are in danger. I think we can both give, in order to preserve our coexistence." The King spoke not wanting the negotiations wrenched from his hands.

"I am in no doubt that you believe you are willing to give but your perspective is short-sighted. You look only to preservation for the time-being. What will happen when either of our kind is all but extinct and neither is strong enough to defeat nor support the other? There is grave danger in allowing such vulnerability."

"You are referring of course to the Script of Anapa. How can you be so deluded by myths? I cannot imagine such a time will come to pass," the king scoffed.

"I can assure you, the Script is real. The Anapa will return as is foreseen. You lack our single, eternal memory, which proves this history. This is what makes you truly mortal for your lives are preserved only in physical objects, all of which can be distorted or destroyed. This is your weakness and yet it is your strength for you are not bound by what has gone before. You rewrite the future each and every day with every new discovery you make." The Avianou chief gestured to the *Lady Lana*. "We must unite our strengths, learn to live as a single entity. It is our only chance."

The king was not certain whether he should be insulted or flattered, "It is an altruistic dream but I cannot see how our two peoples would ever consent."

"Only the bond of flesh will clear that obstacle."

Mackenzie imagined how that must have sounded to a man who'd prided himself on purity of origin and species; a man who'd shunned any breaches to his royal lines.

"And how do you hope to achieve this?"

"I propose a union, so that we might take only the very best of your kind and of the Avianou. I have yet to take a wife and your daughter is of childbearing age by your standards."

The king's face was pale beyond recognition.

"I see your words are worthless. You have no desire to save yourselves, nor extend our coexistence." The Avianou turned, ruffling his wings ready for flight.

"I accept the terms." King Ruben's voice trailed off.

Just as Mackenzie had almost become to believe that what he was watching was reality, the image before him jerked away and he was swirling through nights and days and then an image of the young Princess Veriam, her belly distended with new life.

"So the Queen was never barren?"

"Not until after I was born. My father saw to that. He did not want to risk the King rescinding his words." Petaxi's voice floated tantalising close to Mackenzie's ear. "I am my mother's only child. I am the only heir to the throne of Acantina and you must see that my place is not usurped. The royal line must be reinstated for there is worse to come and we must be prepared to defend ourselves. The Anapa are close."

Petaxi took Mackenzie's hand once more, but she was no longer leading him through the memories of the ancient past. As often does in a dream, time and space had elapsed to the future and she was walking him up the gangplank of the *Lady Lana*, her talons interlocked with his fingers, her wings rustling through the snow strewn ground with a gentle swish, a fine trail left in their wake. Mackenzie's heart raced.

"Welcome aboard, M'lady," he said, his voice little more than a hoarse whisper.

She bowed lower than seemed possible and when she raised her eyes, her gaze did not leave his.

"Do you know why the symbol of your ship is a winged disc?"

"To symbolise the significance of venturing so far."

"No, it is the ancient symbol of my kind. Our fates have been tied for many years. We cannot survive each without the other, but only in the way in which my father envisaged. You are to be part of that."

Her lips brushed his and his blood pounded in his temple.

Mackenzie felt his head swing hard to the left and hit the sill. He awoke with a start. There was a rush of glacial air surging through the room. He brushed what he had assumed was ice from his hair and clothes, realizing too late that it was shattered glass.

Clawing his senses back through the fog of the Harrakuppa, he saw Eidenbury sprawled on the floor of the private room, in a pool of blood, and then a sturdy man was advancing on him, his fists clasped around the compressed steam gyro blaster that must have left the gaping hole in Eidenbury.

"What are you planning with that abomination?" the man demanded, as he sandwiched Mackenzie's head between the brand hot barrel of the blaster and the gritty glass ledge.

Without considering the consequences, Mackenzie put his hand on the weapon to wrest it away. The fluttering shred of teal feather snagged in the ragged glass was all that he needed to give him a resurgence of strength.

With one swift move, he swung his legs up and pushed his assailant out of the broken window.

"Petaxi?" His voice was raw in the freezing air.

With his fingers on the shattered glass, he stared over the ledge after the assassin. To his relief, there was only one corpse smashed on the rocks. He took a deep breath and then hollered again; this time there was no question in his tone.

"Captain Mackenzie." Above, in the swirling wraiths of snow, he could just make out Petaxi's form in flight. She was headed for the *Lady Lana*.

With the assassin's gyro blaster in his hand he dropped down close to the floor in case there were more intruders outside the room. Now Eidenbury was dead, Odan Mackenzie was sworn to protect the princess with the oath he had taken earlier.

He paused at the door, but there was only silence ahead. Stealthily ascending the three steps and traversing the corridor, Mackenzie remained alert to sounds of attack. He met none.

After snapping the safety on and concealing the weapon inside his jacket, he reclaimed his helmet, goggles, and coat from the valet. His bill, he was assured, had already been settled. Without letting on that he was fleeing a murder scene he left the Den as hastily as possible and climbed the docking mast where the *Lady Lana* was moored.

Petaxi was waiting for him, her golden, Avianou flesh impervious to the cold, her feathers ruffling in the stiff blasts of air that gusted off the peak of Mount Oliana. It was as he'd seen in his vision; she took him by the hand and he welcomed her aboard the airship.

"Where to? M'Lady?"

"We must go to Gaskell City - it is under greater threat than humankind can imagine. The army must be mobilised, for we are not fighting the war that everyone thinks we are."

In the blizzard there were hazards Mackenzie did not want to contemplate. His crew snapped to duty immediately. If the captain said they were to depart in treacherous conditions then that is what they would do.

Opening the pump valves the honeycomb ballonets emptied to form the quartet of vacuums that would provide the lift. With the mooring lines released, the *Lady Lana*'s magnificent form lurched away from the docking mast towards the peak.

The Princess gasped.

"Have no fear. Just as you are accustomed to soaring on those gorgeous wings of yours, so I am at controlling the *Lady Lana*." And as if he had known it would happen so the updraft coming from the mountain peak lifted them high into the air, away from the lethal crags of Mount Oliana up through the storm towards the sun beyond the clouds.

"I was not party to Mr Eidenbury's plans. What is your intention now?" Mackenzie asked as he set the coordinates for Gaskell City before turning to Petaxi.

"We are to enter the palace and gain control. The Avianou have mobilised and should be here any moment." She stared out into the vast ocean of cloud, "What if my inheritance is denied? What if they attack the ship before I even show my face?"

"The ship will not be attacked. It is the only ozone tanker and as such, too precious an asset. In that, Eidenbury was most correct in his assessment. As for being accepted, you have Queen Veriam's distinctive nose and brow. There will, no doubt, be those who wish to discredit you, but you must not show weakness or uncertainty for they will use that against you."

That Petaxi did not answer, Mackenzie took her silence for her assent, but then she released a gasp which was followed by Mr. Grazenby's cries of warning.

"On the starboard bow sir! On a collision course!"

"What in creation?" Mackenzie stared at the advancing battalion. Scores of glittering ships were approaching in tight formation.

"I'm guessing they're not the Avianou."

"It is happening."

"What?"

"The Script of Anapa. They are coming to reap the spoils of city."

"The relic your father—"

"Warned my Grandfather of? Yes."

"But that is myth."

"Is it?" Petaxi turned to the brimming horizon.

The golden ships were close enough for Mackenzie to see their canine headed pilots through his telescope.

"Descend!"

With Mackenzie's order given, the vacuum chamber pumps were reversed, flooding the ballonets with air. Reliant on a dainty balance between gravity and buoyancy, the *Lady Lana* started her descent into the steaming depths of Gaskell City.

"I'm afraid they will follow us to the palace," said Petaxi.

"I'm banking on it." Mackenzie smiled at her grimly.

"I don't understand."

"Although the palace is defended by dynamite guns, they will not dare attack the *Lady Lana*, even though she will be coming in unscheduled. To lose the *Lady Lana* will be a death blow for humanity. It will take months to construct another tanker and there just aren't enough materials, or money in Acantina to buy them. And even if there were, there wouldn't be enough time; we would die before completing construction. So we will be safe. As for the Anapa fleet on our tail, it will be a different story."

"That is all you are banking on?"

"The situation is dire here. Do you really have no idea what kingdom you have inherited?" Mackenzie gestured to the viewing gallery.

Petaxi shook her head, her feathers ruffling, and moved towards the window. Mackenzie was not lying. It was no wonder that the rebels had gained a foothold. Once beautiful avenues of trees had become skeletal caricatures of their past. Tents lined the sidewalks and the parklands of parched grass. Dust rose in clouds tainting the atmosphere. Below her, the citizens dawdled along, head shrouded in masks and eyes protected from the dust by thick goggles. The spires of gleaming marble and iron, that had made Gaskell City worthy of the title capital, were sand-blasted and corroded like the rocky canyons to the west. Even the palace, the crowning glory of Acantina, had been eroded; its glistening marble spires no more impressive than the yellowed teeth in the proud smile of an old warrior. The only things that gleamed were the dynamite guns placed strategically around the walls.

"The scripts tell that the Anapa will come to reap the spoils of broken nations, but this," she gestured to Gaskell city below. "I had no idea,"

"You have not chosen to claim the throne at the most propitious time, that is true, but you will succeed." Mackenzie reassured her.

Once the *Lana Lady* aligned with the docking masts of the Queen's Palace, the steam operated hydraulic shield automatically slid up and over the ship, one protective segment at a time and not a moment too soon. The dynamite guns swivelled and tilted to the skies too late to catch the Anapa craft before the first barrage began. The whole palace trembled.

Mackenzie pulled Petaxi down through the deck to the cargo hold where his crew were struggling to lower the long pipes through which the Ozone would be funnelled to the city's hydraulic filtration system. The faster it was removed from the vicinity the less chance there was of the whole load igniting.

Mr. Grazenby tipped his hat as they passed but turned back to his station as another rocket blast rattled the shield. Petaxi stifled a scream and pulled her wings up to protect her back whilst she put her hands over her head.

Mackenzie brought her straight into the palace through the pilot's private entrance.

Guards were waiting for them, fearful that perhaps the *Lady Lana* had been skyjacked.

"Halt! What is your business here?"

"Do you dare question your Queen?"

Mackenzie stared in disbelief at the authority with which Petaxi spoke.

The guard looked uncertain. He turned to Captain Mackenzie for confirmation all the while taking in Petaxi's hybrid features.

Mackenzie gave the slightest nod. The guard hastily bowed down. "Your Majesty,"

Another blast threw a cloud of plaster and dust over them.

"Report to me in the throne room and bring me your commanding officer; I need maps and coordinates." She turned to Mackenzie. "Come. We have a nation to defend."

N.O.A. Rawle regularly burns the midnight oil to get the world in her head in print. A Brit located in Thessaly, her work appears in numerous anthologies and magazines in print and on the web.

For more information, find her at www.noarawle.blogspot.gr, follow her on Twitter @N.O.A.Rawle and like her on Facebook as N.O.A Rawle.

THE JACKALOPE BANDIT

DAVID LEE SUMMERS

WITH A RESOUNDING THUD, the jackalope harvester landed on the boardwalk outside the Santa Fe Railroad depot in Lamy, New Mexico. Its pistons squeaked and hissed as it hopped through the open door into the waiting area. Even Bart Rafferty, the Pinkerton detective assigned to the railroad, smiled at the man-sized machine that resembled an overgrown jack rabbit with antennae shaped like antelope horns between its ears. He figured some local farmer had allowed the harvester to run away from him.

Out of place as the machine looked in a rail depot, they seemed little better in farmers' fields. A professor at the College of Agriculture and Mechanic Arts designed the rabbit-like automata to hop through fields, collect fruit or vegetables with their mechanical forelimbs, and shove them into their mouths as though eating. Bins in the creatures' bellies collected the harvest. A farmer could control a herd of jackalope harvesters with a wireless control unit. Useful as the jackalopes could be, a field full of them always made Rafferty think the farmer had been beset by a plague of mechanical vermin.

Despite his amusement, Rafferty tried not to be distracted. He was on the lookout for Tom Ketchum, wanted for bank and train robbery. At one point, Rafferty thought he saw Ketchum, but the man just lowered his hat and left the depot without making any trouble.

The harvester stood in the empty waiting area for a moment, its ears swiveling back and forth on bearings, before it hopped over to the payroll window. That's when Rafferty finally noticed the jackalope held an Army Colt six-shooter in its mechanical claw. It lifted the gun and its mouth fell open. "Bring the payroll."

The clerk behind the window stepped back, whether from the shock of the eerie, disembodied voice that came from a normally mute harvester, or the six-gun pointed at him, Rafferty wasn't sure. Either way, the detective took action. He drew his own six-gun and stepped forward.

The jackalope's torso swirled around, while the face continued to stare at the befuddled clerk. "Stay where you are," said the strange, mechanical voice.

"Drop your gun," called Rafferty.

The jackalope lowered its gun slightly. Just when Rafferty thought the gun would clatter to the wooden floor, it discharged, sending a bullet right between Rafferty's feet. The jackalope lifted the revolver. "The next shot goes between your eyes, Pink. Even if you shoot first, the bullet will probably just ricochet off my steel frame."

Rafferty ground his teeth, but finally dropped his own revolver, figuring it might buy him time to find another course of action.

The jackalope's gun whirled around and aimed at the clerk again. "The payroll."

The clerk brought over a chest, which had just arrived on the afternoon train.

"Open it and place the money on the counter," ordered the jackalope.

The clerk began placing stacks of bills on the counter in front of the machine. With its free hand, the jackalope grabbed the stacks and shoved them into its mouth, where they dropped into the storage container in its belly, just like a harvest of fruit or vegetables.

Rafferty crept forward while the jackalope faced the clerk. Its ears swiveled again. Just as Rafferty reached out to grab the jackalope's revolver, the mechanical beast's torso whirled again, sending Rafferty sprawling across the floor and knocking his bowler hat clean off.

The jackalope finished swallowing the payroll, then turned and hopped from the depot. Rafferty sprang to his feet, retrieved his hat, and ran after the mechanical creature. Once he reached the street, it was nowhere to be seen. The detective couldn't hear anything either. Across the street an airship's propellers spun to life at the new aerodrome. No tracks showed in the hard-packed dirt of the street between the two buildings either.

Rafferty cursed under his breath as the airship lifted into the air.

A tip-tapping from the new telegraph unit on the corner of her writing bureau startled Marshal Larissa Seaton of Mesilla, New Mexico. She hadn't yet grown used to having the device on her desk. She leaned forward and acknowledged the signal, using the new-fangled three-key telegraph system Professor Maravilla had installed for her.

The telegraph tapped away, disgorging a ribbon of paper with holes. The marshal was glad she didn't have to try to listen to the taps. She never decoded messages very fast. She scanned the holes in the ribbon and transcribed the letters onto a notepad. A Pinkerton detective named Rafferty, assigned to the Santa Fe railroad asked if she was the woman marshal who solved crazy mysteries, such as the giant wasps of San Antonio and the time Curly Bill Bresnahan robbed a bank in Tucson with a giant mining machine. She acknowledged that she helped solve both cases.

The telegraph sprang to life again. As Larissa transcribed the letters, her eyes widened. The message detailed a series of robberies taking place around the state. The Pinkerton detective had been present for the first one. In each case, a mechanical jackalope harvester had demanded money and escaped soon after. He asked for her help.

She sent back a brief acknowledgement saying she would do what she could. She opened a drawer and retrieved a map of the state. Carrying it over to a table, she unrolled it and looked at the locations where the robberies occurred. Only one was a rail payroll. The second was a bank robbery in Roswell and the third involved a new-fangled motor stage in Socorro. Sheriff Elfego Baca had been called right away, but the jackalope vanished before his arrival.

There were two common elements. A jackalope harvester always committed the crime and the crime's location was never far from an airfield. Larissa decided to pay a visit to the local airfield and pick up some timetables, then go visit the man who invented the jackalope harvesters.

Larissa walked a few streets over to where Professor M.K. Maravilla kept a home near the newly opened College of Agriculture and Mechanic Arts. "Ah, Larissa, so good to see you!" he said when he opened the door. "I was just making tea. Would you care for some?"

"That would be lovely, thank you," said Larissa.

He invited her in and she hung the army captain's hat she affected on a rack by the door. The professor then led her to his den and indicated she should sit while he continued through the house to the kitchen. Shelves lined the professor's den. Most were covered with books, but a few held working scale models of the professor's inventions.

Instead of sitting, Larissa strolled over to a shelf that held a miniature version of the ornithopters he built to study owls, but proved instrumental in overthrowing the Russian airship invasion. Alongside it stood a model of the javelina mining machine, which the Apaches had adapted into battle wagons and still used to give the army trouble in Arizona Territory.

There was even a miniature jackalope, like the one Detective Rafferty purported was behind the bank robberies around the state.

A moment later, Professor Maravilla appeared in the doorway, holding two cups of tea. "Admiring my collection?" he asked.

She reached out and took a cup and saucer. "Quite a set of accomplishments." She lifted the cup and took a sip, then moved over to an armchair. "Those jackalope harvesters you designed. They require an operator don't they? They're not like the Japanese automata that have an onboard Babbage engine that can be programmed for a set of actions."

Maravilla took a sip of tea, then chuckled and shook his head. "No, no. If I put a Babbage engine in a jackalope, it would never have room to carry the harvest. That's why they have the antennas on their head." He waggled his fingers over his head as he took a seat across from the marshal. "They allow an operator to send wireless signals to the harvester and control its operation."

"Have you heard about the string of robberies involving jackalope harvesters?"

The professor narrowed his gaze and set his cup on a table beside him. "No, please tell me more."

Larissa filled him in on the information Detective Rafferty had telegraphed. "Each of the robberies was just before a Texas and Territorial Airship was scheduled to depart nearby. They're a small cargo line that occasionally takes on a few passengers and has stops in West Texas along with the New Mexico and Arizona Territories."

"You think one of their crewmembers is responsible?"

"Or a regular passenger. I just need a way to get some evidence that will stand up in court." She lifted the tea and took a sip.

"I think I can do better than that, I think I can help you catch the fiend who has purloined one of my jackalopes and put it to such nefarious use."

Larissa smiled. "That's what I hoped, professor. Can you have something ready in three days?"

"Why so soon?"

Larissa sipped her tea again as she considered what she knew. "There's a bank next to the airfield in Mesilla Park. If I'm right about the pattern, that's where our jackalope will strike next." Horses were outlawed on the streets of Mesilla. The adjoining town of Mesilla Park had grown up as a sort of transportation hub where people could stable their animals and find other forms of transportation.

The professor ran his finger over the hairs of his thin, immaculate mustache. "I know enough not to question your hunches. It's a tall order, but I think I can have something ready."

Larissa took another sip of tea, then excused herself to telegraph a message to Detective Rafferty.

Larissa Seaton hung back in the shadows of the Farmer's Bank and Trust in Mesilla Park. Earlier that day, she warned the bank president that a robbery was likely and that tellers should simply cooperate. She had a plan to recover the funds. The president eyed her skeptically. Her reputation as a marshal who accomplished amazing things preceded her, but she was still a woman promising things he would be concerned about a man being able to deliver. Still, he reluctantly agreed.

As expected, the Texas & Territorial Airship *Yellow Rose* landed in the afternoon. Despite that, Larissa's stomach churned. Was she right about the connection between the robberies and the airship route? Had she picked the next target correctly? Had everything happened that would allow her plan to go forward? She'd carried out her part, but a lot could still go wrong.

The afternoon wore on. At one point, a man in a black hat exited and left the door standing wide open. She was about to go close the door when she heard the thudding and wheezing that accompanied a jackalope harvester. It landed on the boardwalk outside and came through the door. She almost breathed a sigh of relief.

The jackalope's mouth dropped open and a cold, hard voice spoke. "Everyone drop to the floor." The jackalope's torso whirled around, revealing that the automaton carried an Army Colt revolver. To indicate he was serious, the jackalope aimed the weapon at the ceiling and fired a shot. Plaster rained down from above and people dove to the floor, Larissa included.

She watched as the jackalope hopped over to the teller and demanded that he deliver a stack of money. The teller scrambled to do as instructed. The harvester ingested all the money and then hopped over to the next window. Right as it finished with the second stack, Larissa stood, took quick aim with a derringer she'd had concealed in her sleeve and fired. The bullet penetrated the jackalope's outer skin with a thud, causing it to rock backward. For a moment, she thought it would topple over, but it recovered its balance.

She dove to the floor again as it whirled around and fired. The shot went over her head. Without collecting any more money, the jackalope hopped out of the bank. Larissa jumped to her feet and followed it outside. She watched it hop across to the aerodrome. Fifteen minutes later, the *Yellow Rose* lifted into the sky. She watched it and hoped everything was in place and Professor Maravilla's idea would work as expected.

Detective Rafferty hadn't known what to make of the package that arrived at his rooming house in Santa Fe the day before. It contained a device that looked a little like a compass, except that it had a toggle switch for power and a miniature Tesla gas tube in the top that didn't seem to do anything. What's more the needle remained locked in one position.

In the package with the strange device was a ticket for the Texas and Territorial airship *Yellow Rose*, plus a hastily written letter from Marshal Larissa Seaton explaining that all of this would somehow help him capture the person committing robberies with a mechanical jackalope.

He waited aboard the *Yellow Rose* while it sat docked at Mesilla Park. As the airship lifted off, he took out the strange compass-like device and turned it on as instructed in the letter. This time, the dial whirled around and the Tesla gas tube began a slow, rhythmic red pulse. The detective's eyebrows came together and he stepped out into the corridor. The arrow remained fixed on the ship's stern hold and the light pulsed a little faster. It seemed to indicate he should go that direction. He strode down the corridor toward the hold.

As he walked, the Tesla tube's pulsations increased, as though encouraging him to keep going. The detective's heart raced. He wished he had his six-gun, but the steward made him check the weapon when he boarded due to the dangers of sparks and weapon discharges aboard an airship that used hydrogen as a lifting gas.

Rafferty opened the door to the hold and found himself face-to-face with the jackalope. Its front hatch was open and Ol' Tom Ketchum stood before it, lifting out stacks of money.

"So you're behind the robberies after all, eh, Tom?"

Ketchum dropped the money, reached over and grabbed the Army Colt from the jackalope's claw and aimed it at Rafferty. "Lotta good that'll do ya', Pink," said the outlaw.

"You're not going to fire," said Rafferty, tucking the handy tracking device in his coat pocket. "If I understand right, you'll cause this whole ship to go up like a candle."

"Only if I ignite the hydrogen," said Ketchum with a sneer. "Down here in the gondola, that's not a big risk."

Just then, the jackalope's mouth fell open. For a moment, it sounded like the mechanical contrivance cleared its throat, then it spoke with a woman's voice. "Let's see if I've got this working right. If you can hear me, this is Larissa Seaton. I've been listening to everything you've been saying. I suggest you take a look out the nearest starboard porthole."

Ketchum took two steps backward and looked over his shoulder while keeping the six-gun aimed at Rafferty. He gasped.

Rafferty took a chance and stepped to a porthole immediately to his left. Outside, flying alongside the airship was a craft that flapped its wings like a bird. In the middle of the body sat a pilot. On the bird's back, some kind of gun was aimed at the airship. Rafferty recognized the flapping craft as one of the army's ornithopters, developed during the Russian war.

"That bullet I fired into the jackalope in Mesilla Park lodged into the device's metal frame. According to Professor Maravilla, it has electronics on it that allow me hear what you're saying and I gather you can hear me ... just like you can project your voice through the jackalope, Mr. Ketchum."

"That's a mighty cute trick, l'il missy," said Ketchum. "I've got my gun on the Pink here, so don't you try no funny business."

"Sorry, I forgot to properly introduce myself. I'm *Marshal* Larissa Seaton," came the voice from the jackalope. "I also heard what you said about not being worried about igniting the airship's hydrogen with your six-gun. That makes sense. What you should worry about is that I can ignite your airship's hydrogen very nicely with my Edison Gun."

Rafferty's gut clenched and his eyes drifted toward the ceiling. Even though she was a woman, the marshal had a reputation for taking whatever action she felt necessary to finish a job.

Ketchum laughed at Rafferty's reaction. "The Pink will burn if you do."

Rafferty swallowed, then gathered his resolve. "Don't worry about me. Do what you need to."

"I won't fire the Edison Gun unless you shoot Mr. Rafferty," said Larissa. "At that point, I don't think he'll care much what happens to the airship."

Ketchum frowned. "What do you want me to do?"

"Land at the next aerodrome and surrender yourself to me. If you do, I'll make sure you get a fair trial." Larissa paused as though considering. "Hand your gun over to Mr. Rafferty."

"You know," said Ketchum, "I seem to remember those ornithopters use a lot of fuel and don't have anywhere near the range of an airship. I'm willing to bet we can stay up here a lot longer than you can."

Rafferty suspected the outlaw was right, but he suddenly realized if Seaton could speak through the jackalope, she might be able to control it as well. "So what are you going to do?" he asked. "Stand there, at the second porthole from the back, holding me at gunpoint for several hours until the marshal gives up?"

Just then, the jackalope hopped forward into Ketchum. The impact knocked the outlaw out. "You got 'em, Marshal Seaton." Rafferty cast about and found a coil of rope. He hogtied Ketchum, then stood. "Time for me to talk to the pilots. You think they know what's going on?"

"I doubt it. Ketchum was a paying passenger, posing as a jackalope salesman."

"Thank you kindly for your help, ma'am."

"My pleasure," said Larissa. Outside, the ornithopter veered off. "Let me know if you have any more interesting cases, though. This was fun."

Rafferty removed his bowler hat and scratched his head, thinking her idea of fun didn't exactly match his. Nevertheless, he was grateful for new friends.

David Lee Summers is the author of ten novels and numerous short stories and poems. His novels include *Owl Dance*, a wild west steampunk adventure which tells the story of a microscopic alien swarm manipulating events in 1877 New Mexico, and *The Solar Sea* which imagines the first voyage to the outer planets aboard a solar sail spacecraft. His short stories and poems have appeared in such magazines and anthologies as *Realms of Fantasy, Cemetery Dance,* and *Human Tales.* In addition to writing, David edited the quarterly science fiction and fantasy magazine *Tales of the Talisman* for ten years and has edited three science fiction anthologies: *A Kepler's Dozen, Space Pirates* and *Space Horrors.* When not working with the written word, David operates telescopes at Kitt Peak National Observatory.

Learn more about David at *davidleesummers.com*

AFTER THE CATASTROPHE: THE LADY OF CASTLE ROCK

STEVE MOORE

THE EARTH COOLED AND VOLCANOES emerged as hot spots on the thin crusts of existence. The levels of Oxygen and Hydrogen meant water existed and Planet Earth was in the perfect orbit for it to remain liquid and flow then change into gaseous form and fall as rain. Basic amino acids formed due to the electrical storms associated with Volcanism and life came into being, but it would be years before sentient life would emerge.

The spirits of imagination need a canvas to paint upon and as time passed by several sparks formed a way to communicate through the aether. There were many junctures and crossroads in time when they would come together. In Greece they were at the Symposium. There were philosophers, male and female, trying to understand life. In sixteenth century Southwark, South London, Olde England they met to write plays and express emotion to a wider audience through sonnets and pamphlets.

The spirits took different forms: There was a sea captain with a walrus moustache who travelled the World and had visited the Colonies, a lady of noble blood who enjoyed mixing with the low life of Southwark. There was Emma Otana, the draper's daughter, with an unsurpassed and earthy imagination, Young Maxwell of Norfolk, Will Jackspear and Daffyd Winwinter of New Spain. They were close friends who gathered in the alehouse and spoke of many things about the world, about life, love and imagination. Later these spirits reformed in the Victorian age in the salons of Paris where they argued with Zola in their quest to enlighten with the written word. Then one of these spirits, wearing a pith helmet, gold patterned waistcoat and the well-cut brown uniform of the Imperial Camel Corps walked into the current manifestation of their communion. They had been at turns The Writer's Emporium, The Scribes Arms, The Crossed Pens, The Inn of the Seven Poets and The House of the Written Word. They were now the Scribblers' Den.

He removed his pith helmet and handed over his basic weapons, two black-powder Remington revolvers, to Maxwell who handed over a buff numbered ticket 69. "Ah, my lucky number."

"Welcome Staff Sergeant, better keep that comment in the Armory. Any luck?" asked Maxwell.

The reply was; "Good point old son. Well there were a couple of hopefuls who might complete a novel and a beautiful American lady, tall, dressed in white, who might be a poet but she never seems to write down her amazing use of the language. It's such a shame." He smiled and walked through the main saloon doors of the Denizen's Arms to join the Scribbler's Den. There was a wooden shingle sign hanging down that said "Jack's Rule's apply within, but all writers are welcome; 'Be nice or else.'"

Inside, the wallpaper was red with a gold embossed pattern. There was a gold dado rail and the wall was painted dark green under that. The floor was dark polished wood parquet, there were easy chairs and sofas, and on the walls were illustrations of airships, views of Africa, and San Diego Harbor. The lighting was soft gaslight and the Doobie Brothers played Listen to the Music, in the background. Polishing the spotless mahogany bar on the left hand side of the room was Jack himself. On the right was the fireplace with iron pokers and coal scuttles, firedogs, and a screen. There were horse brasses on the wall and a gleaming cavalry sabre bolted over the mantle. Jack was wearing his cap and goggles and was one hell of an author. Katie sat at the far end of the bar, slender, intelligent, telling Jack, "You should not use mahogany in this place as you are exacerbating the demise of the rainforest and life on earth". She paused. "If only there was an Atlantis," she mused. She was resplendent in green satin and her gold hexagonal glasses.

Jack looked at her sideways and quipped; "Well God gives and God takes away, Lady." She drank down her Martini and rustled off into a corner of the room where she was painting some architectural designs for a vast library.

"Hi Sarge - what will it be?" asked Jack. "I will have a pint of London Pride please, Jack."

"What?" Jack snapped.

"It's a bitter ale made by Fuller's of London," the sergeant replied.

Jack retorted "You Brits can be a pain sometimes with your warm beer. If you did not love Texas so much I would throw you out."

"Yes Jack, it is your prerogative, sir".

The sergeant turned as another figure entered the bar.

"Hey Sarge, what's happening?" It was Will Jackspear. Will was tall, dark and holding a folder full of pages with line after line of words. Jack placed the bitter beer on a coaster.

"Will - you *are* a star. It looks like another novella in the making."

"Yes, bro, a 20,000-word novella and cruising to a full novel in a week or two. Ouch".

"What's the matter, Will?" asked Jack.

"Dentistry is killing me, but the Novocaine is making my imagination expand!" He laughed. "You take care matey." Will turned to Jack and ordered a Malawi Shandy, one of Jack's specials.

There was a stiff swish of taffeta as Lady Naomi entered the room, wearing a dark maroon dress with cream satin bows, her long golden hair cascading down from her matching maroon hat. Decorated with long black feathers and black lace, it was ever so raggamuffinly askew. Following her in a French Colonial Service pith helmet, bush jacket, and matching khaki skirt, was Alice De Cody. Alice was a dispossessed marchioness, doomed to travel the planet in search of her lost bears that had escaped in the Caribbean while en-route to Yellowstone National Park.

"Hi Sarge" she smiled.

"Hi Alice. Hope you come to England soon." The ladies ordered a bottle of wine and a bottle of still water and sat down together at the bar beside Icky, the Lord of Temperance in a brown bowler hat, who frowned at the wine but helped himself to the mineral water.

"I'm here to avoid rabid squirrels, ladies" he smiled.

Then young Bryce, wearing a brass engraved monocular lens, stepped up to the bar and poured another absinthe, which he kindly proffered to the sergeant. Despite the stupidity of mixing absinthe with beer, the sergeant drank and drank and the evening flew by.

There was David "The Top Hat" expounding on the latest gas analysis technologies in astronomy with Lady Naomi and her nail-gun-wielding friend Emma Hampshire. Then into the Den appeared the dark lady all in black twirling her black parasol. The sergeant's heart thumped faster and he drank more.

Many conversations later the sergeant found himself slumped in his favorite chair, the red leather one by the fire. The fire was now roaring bright yellow and red as Jack changed the music to Steely Dan.

Perhaps because the last conversation he could remember was Lady Naomi talking about how crass dream scenes in literature and drama were, he found himself fading away into the world of Morpheus and Greek myths. Then Lady Naomi was asking questions. The dark lady of his dreams still twirled a black parasol and stared at him.

Then he recalled his meeting with that fine-featured American lady in white, who might be a writer raced through his mind and slowly his eyes flickered closed and he was in America flying high above a decimated landscape. He found himself telling a story in a stream of green absinthe-induced unconsciousness.

"Catastrophe is a Greek word," he began, "along with chaos and anarchy.

The world suffered all of these maladies when in 1929, in this time stream, the warring armies of Europe developed small nuclear devices. They already had biological and chemical weapons and they had converted vast autonomous airships to carry these weapons of impure destruction, far and wide and indiscriminately. They commenced a hell driven destruction and in their hubris they used dirty warfare. That rendered the surface of the Earth either a vast sheet of black vitreous glass or a collection of massive piles of rubble where only mould and fungus survived and little else prospered. The political world quickly fell apart as did all human society. Far into the middle of America where the plains and the Rocky Mountains jostled for dominance, a rock loomed over the destroyed landscape. Legend has it that it was once called Castle Rock and was located in the American state of Colorado, once twinned with El Dorado, the city of gold. It was just south of the once populous metropolis of Envy, USA." The sergeant dreamed.

A bright golden ball of benign nuclear power arose over the American plains. The vast skies of Colorado shone blue and white. Gray lilac cloudscapes were dappled onto God's great canvas by his paintbrush, random and creative. Where the Sun kissed the clouds He painted fine lines of pink fire. It was still cold so early in the morning. The beautiful survivor, clad in white, was known as the baroness of Castle Rock. She was a member of one of America's ruling families. Now she looked through her great brass optical periscope system from a chamber located in natural caverns, deep in the centre of the towering rock. From this ancient control room she slowly scanned the surface. This observation chamber is part of her home. Part of the cavern complex where she had played as a child and, since the catastrophe, where her family always lived. She could remember being led into the depths as a little girl and that last glimpse of the surface as her father closed the airlock doors. When she closed her eyes she could recall the screaming, the roar of pounding, scraping, tears and shouting of those unfortunates that could not afford anti-contamination suits, rubberized helmets, and filters, suddenly muffled. Then there was the terrible silence. They were doomed. They had not been selected for survival. She felt deep melancholy as she thought *there were children out there* and now they were just dust, random atoms of carbon, traces of water and calcium. The electric spark of life now dissipated but hopefully their spirits were now flown away to heaven safe from this man made Earthly hell. The Baroness sighed as that silence echoed in her memory.

The baroness was ash blonde, willowy, and possessed a natural grace. Her eyes were bright chips of grey azure that match the Colorado skies and always belied her amusement. She wore her white rubber ceremonial pencil dress that clung to her honed body as a second skin. Her blue-grey eyes blinked at the bright sunlight as she slowly introduced circular filters and adjusted the magnification of her periscope system. She scanned the horizon to search for mythical airships, metal crawlers, bird-craft, for anything. Microphones on the surface played the mournful sound of the wind into her headphones. She looked and listened out of sheer habit but today her expectation had changed.

Last night she had experienced vivid dreams. In her vision she was wearing her white cotton dress, but amazingly, that was all. Where was the latex suit or the birdlike respirator?

She walked on green grass that tickled between her toes. The grass was wet with heavy morning dew. The trees all around her were tall and green and she heard bird song and then there was a voice. A clear voice had spoken to her; *Explore. Push the limits. The time is now. Only you can do this. Explore.*

The baroness woke and unzipped her sleeping pod. Beads of sweat had formed on her brow and she was breathing heavily. She drank a small glass of water and waited for the sun to rise. Later, in her observation room, she slowly smoothed her rubber dress, running her thin but strong hands over the shiny surface. She self-consciously realized with a smile that her nipples were now pert. The moisture of her perspiration made her rubber dress slightly uncomfortable to wear, but she actually liked that negative tension. The baroness knew she was very lucky. She was a member of the old aristocracy of Colorado and enjoyed many privileges far beyond the lot of the ordinary hoi polloi survivors.

After the Catastrophe, people had chiseled underground railways wherever possible, making the land of America a Swiss cheese of tunnels and caverns. Colorado's long history of mining silver, gold, copper, and zinc had provided a head start in this region. Humans barely survived underground, living on edible moulds and fungi. Some fruits were grown under artificial lights and in some places there were glass roofs that risked baring themselves to the real Sun. "Meat" was mostly reconstituted slugs, snails, or worm meal from deep caverns where humans disposed of their dead. This means of recycling provided a way around the still strong taboo of cannibalism.

The baroness slammed the handles into the periscope body. The periscope rose to sit neatly in the ceiling. She changed into a black latex suit and wore a white cotton dress as well. Although it wasn't strictly necessary, she pulled onto her face her cherished black respirator. A respirator was a habit underground in the caverns and one only removed it for intimacy, but only when totally relaxed and trusting. There were still occasional outbreaks of anti-human virus and one could not be too careful outside of collective protection. The State Detector Corps provided regular reports on contaminant levels and red-carded out of bounds areas that were building up to dangerous levels according to their sensors. Their electric screens proclaimed publicly the alert state in bright green signage and that also helped keep the populace of Sub-Terranea fully informed and prepared. The alert state was moderate risk. The decontaminators would soon spray and scrub every passage with strong bleach and biocides.

In another time stream a man would walk on the moon. Here a man walking on the Earth was an even more ambitious desire. People communicated by dispatch papers. These were the collected gossip and stories of life and death which were recycled in the papers over many editions. After a while only the same few stories circulated, as not much happened that was so different under the surface of America.

The baroness turned to find the tunnel that led to the Dragon Hall of the Castle Rock community of Sub-Terranea West Central. It was almost time for the conclave. It is now many years since the hiatus and the flight to the depths. In America an uncounted population of survivors kept humanity preserved in aspic whilst Europe was a vast plain of bone, ash, and tachylite. The Eiffel tower survived it seems but elsewhere the museums, galleries, and railway stations were burnt out piles of rubble. Mountains once tall and proud were pummeled to dust by nuclear chain reactions and the following clouds of biological hazard. The Sahara was a vast natural firebreak that protected Southern and equatorial Africa but clouds of bio death occasionally passed south on the winds to wreak havoc.

Deep in the African mountains gorillas were prospering, as man died off and the rainforests expanded. A jealous and dying European sent all remaining airships on a course of destruction that tore apart much of the United States. He laughed as he coughed up blood and died in a mess of involuntary twitches.

In the Castle Rock the lady baroness drank some water and savored every drop. She then made her way to the Hall of Purity where the morning conclave was held. All the officers and people of Castle Rock were there, all 287 of them. They sang songs of praise and arias to God and then the national anthem. Then it was time to speak.

"Brethren, I want to explore the surface," the baroness said softly.

"You cannot be serious, Lady. This is ill-timed and a perverse humor, Baroness." The long respirator of the magister turned away from her as the people formed a circle in the Dragon hall. Tall mock windows let artificial light into this chamber deep underground.

"You know I am serious," she replied with a hint of annoyance. "I always am. As to timing and my sense of humor I would have thought you had read my profile." She paused, breathed in deeply, and softened her tone. "I have just felt a calling. A voice from the aether is telling me I am selected as special and my destiny is to explore."

The baroness shook her long hair to let it fall behind her shoulders. Her respirator lenses reflected the colors of the stained glass and her eyes flashed. The magister turned to the top hatted Seneschal who, in a deep sonorous voice said;

"The word *explore* is banned. I cannot believe you uttered it. According to the Litany, chapter 24, verse four and I quote: 'Do not explore. To explore is death,' at least that is what I recall." The seneschal looked sadly at the baroness.

She said, "I know and understand the rules stated in the Litany but the imagery I have received in my vision is compelling; lakes of water, green fields, and children running free. I saw families enjoying the lake, enjoying the surface."

"Blasphemy!" came his reply. "You may be a baroness but you cannot express these wild dreams publicly. The people might listen and be killed. We need a critical mass of population to survive. If they are lured away from home by your fanciful, crazy dreams it will be the end of us all."

The baroness knew he would have spat into his respirator at that point as he shouted these words at her. She could only guess what he looked like out of his mouse-eyed respirator with two inch brown lenses and rubberized cotton which formed his traditional mask. A black and khaki tube extended to his large round filter box.

"Now cease this talk of madness. The service continues."

Anonymous humans in respirators and rubber or rubberized materials shared contact. Often intimately as they brushed up against each other, mingling and sharing the privilege of survival. It was a bonding ceremony with sexual overtones. Beneath the rubber age, gender, race, religion, beauty or disfigurement did not matter. Survival equipment to a certain extent made everyone equal, totally equal, if one had the same kit to the same capability. The baroness then thought *Perhaps this blight on humanity is a good thing?* As a hand brushed her body here and she caressed someone elsewhere. The clockwork gramophone played the National Anthem again to bring this conclave to an end. After the mingling they departed the temple via one of the seven doors. The eighth was marked Citadel.

As the baroness left the hall a figure in black followed her. A male in a modern bird-beaked respirator ran up and said "Greetings Baroness".

"Hello," she replied politely.

"I heard what you said during the service and could not help but overhear what you said to the seneschal. I want to explore as well!" He shocked even himself as he said the "E" word. He seemed to show this surprise as he expressed it. He could almost see the Baroness smiling behind her black respirator; her eyes were bright and shone with acceptance. He was slightly shorter than her but she could see his bright blue eyes through clear eye lenses. There was nothing distinctive about his voice. He might have a slight lisp she thought. So they set off together to explore.

The tunnels were lit by electricity but she knew not where the power came from. The rock had been cut through in these tunnels and in most cases they had been blasted with melt weapons that generated mini nuclear explosions and cut the rock by making it molten like volcanic lava. Deeper they went and travelled further than they each had ever been, far from their area of familiarity or comfort zone. There were side corridors and rooms containing beds and wardrobes with incomprehensible writing on the walls or on posters. "I trust in Nixon," for example or "IRS rules for non-domicile taxation."

The writing was faded and peeling away, as its meaning already had. These were relics that would turn to dust if disturbed. The baroness noticed the tunnels were heading upward when her companion shouted;

"Baroness, Baroness, look over here." There was a shaft heading straight up with ladder rungs set into the structure.

"Shall we?" asked her companion.

"Yes, but what is your name?"

"Remus. I am named after the city of Remulin, in Italy. It was in Europe."

"Remus have your tools readily to hand, we might need our blades." said the baroness.

"Oh Baroness, I could not hurt anyone. I am a passive." The baroness felt a pang of frustration.

"Very well, you had better follow me," she said as she climbed up the shaft. She switched on the battery-powered light in her respirator as she pulled herself up. Black latex suit shining in the light, her white cotton skirts rustling as she climbed ever upwards. Remus in his black suits copied her. His respirator was an older pattern and the lamp was an add-on, not an integral part of the respirator design, however, it did the job and he followed the baroness, admiring her shapely legs as she climbed up ahead of him. After a while she shouted, "Remus, I am at the surface."

He felt a wave of excitement "Great!" he replied.

At the top of the shaft was a large hemispherical area with portholes that shone beams of light into the darkness of the room. At the opposite end of the room was an air lock door. There were dusty tables and chairs and black-crusted computer equipment. Wires and cables and conduits appeared to emerge outside. Instinctively they ran to a porthole. Holding the rim the baroness pulled herself up to look outside. Remus pulled up a box and climbed up to look over her shoulder.

"Oh my God," she said breathlessly. Outside were trees, shrubs, and a small glade with a pond. Nothing like it had been seen since before the catastrophe. The baroness had seen only rock rubble and glass above the ground with her periscope. She had never seen green life above ground. Three locks sealed the door to the air lock. Designated X, Y, and Z the locks were stiff but a club hammer from a box of implements freed the corrosion with little effort. Smudges of brown rust now stained the baroness's dress. She opened the airlock door. It creaked open into another chamber. They entered and shut the door behind them.

"This is it, Remus." The baroness smiled as she opened the final door and walked forward, feeling a great sense of inner turmoil. Remus collapsed on the floor and looked out.

"I can't, I can't, it is too big." His concerns were infectious and the baroness stood still about five paces from the air lock reeling from the vast endless blue skies but also transfixed by the greenery and the soft feel of the yielding grass underfoot. She knelt down and rubbed the grass with her hands, still clad in latex gloves. This was overwhelming but she felt her courage and daring build up. Checking her belt-worn threat detector showed it was still green. The paper test kit that she pulled from another belt pouch was neutral. She slowly removed her respirator breathed in deeply, then thoroughly exhaled. She closed her eyes and waited. Nothing. Relieved that she was still alive, she unzipped her latex suit after letting her cotton dress drop to the ground. Sunshine glowed on her face. The clean air danced over her skin. This was where she belonged. This was natural.

"Baroness, help me. I am afraid," Remus whispered, his respirator muffling his voice.

"Come here Remus," she said kindly, stretching her hand toward him. He unclipped his respirator and, holding the door frame, moved forward out of the shadows.

His face was pale and his eyes dark. "I am not sure I can do this," he said.

"Yes you can," said the baroness warmly. She smiled and stood up. Her confidence grew and she walked around this clearing by a wood. The trees swayed in the slight breeze. She sighed, "Oh my God this is wonderful."

Remus kneeled down and felt the grass.

"Oh my God this *is* wonderful but if we can survive here we have been living a lie. The poisoned land is pure."

"Yes Remus, it is pure," she said.

The door slammed closed. Remus panicked and jumped to his feet as the baroness ran forward to the door and, looking through a porthole saw the familiar respirator of the magister.

"If you go they will all go!" he screamed. "Then what will happen without rules? I will tell you young lady. Society will collapse!"

"Magister, Magister open the door" she shouted. He did not hear. His eyes were rolling at the scene and he retreated into the domed hall. Not sure what to do and beginning to feel scared, the Baroness slammed the club hammer onto the metal wall of the dome's skin and it dented. She slammed it again and the metal stretched and then tore. The metal walls which had protected their community for so long had oxidized over the years. She kept hitting, feeling adrenaline course through her veins as flakes of metal broke off inside the dome and fell to the floor. The magister returned screaming.

"What have you done?" He was distraught. "Our integrity is compromised. No, no, no!" His voice faded as he clambered down the ladder. The baroness and Remus removed a metal panel, walked back into the dome and light flooded in. There was a metal helmet on the floor and what might have been metal runners from a filing cabinet. She picked up the helmet and walked back out through the gap into the open air. A sod of turf was quickly cut and packed into the green rusting helmet. She strapped the helmet to her leather belt then rezipped her suit and filled her pack with material she found in the dome. With the club hammer still in hand, they made their way into the dome and back down the rungs of the ladder. What did she have to do to prove this to the people? Would they listen?

Back on home ground, The baroness took Remus to her private quarters.

"I am going to take a shower," she said quietly. Remus sat down, staring at the sod of grass. She placed the contents of her pack on the table. There was a notebook, several rectangular objects, a rubber glove, glass phials, paper test detectors, a respirator canister, and a ball point pen whose ink had dried out. Remus stared at the items but caught out of the corner of his eye the baroness going into the decontamination shower. He walked over and joined her. They both removed their suits and enjoyed the cleansing water and detergent that cascaded over their bodies. The water stopped and warm air fans took over. They were too pre-occupied to be concerned about their nakedness and the baroness handed a robe to Remus.

Drying her hair with a warm air device, she sat down at the table. Curious about the rectangular object, she picked it up and pressed a green button. It briefly flashed lime green then stopped with a squawking sound. She took another object and saw it was a battery pack with eight batteries in good condition inside. Fitting the batteries into the other object caused it to spring to life. She moved a dial and listened to the static. When she suddenly heard;

"Alpha two two, this is Imperial Angolan Airship Alpha three nine, THE AUGUSTO, do you read me? Over."She was so startled she nearly dropped it. Her eyes widened.

"Hello!" she shouted.

Remus looked awestruck. "That's a radio" he said, clearly amazed. "I thought they were legendary."

"Hello, can you hear me?" said the baroness. Somehow she pressed the talk button.

"Hello unknown station. We are the Imperial Angolan Airship THE AUGUSTO. Where are you?" The radio screeched and then she pressed the talk button again.

"We are living in Castle Rock, Colorado, United States of America." She released the button and the Airship cut in.

"We are off the coast in the Gulf of Texas. Do you require rescue? Our maps indicate you are in poisoned lands."

"We think the land has healed," she replied. "We have grass and trees now."

"We have triangulated your transmission and we are on our way to you," replied the deep, resonant voice. "Stay on this frequency. ETA 72 hours. Is there a readily identifiable landmark?"

"Yes, the Castle Rock itself," she said.

"Roger that. Be seeing you. THE AUGUSTO out."

Wide-eyed and shocked, Remus whispered, "you are going to leave. Don't leave me."

The baroness tenderly caressed his cheek.

"I need to do this. This is the real meaning of the word explore, and I will come back but with broader knowledge of the world. Angolan airships have been mentioned in the surviving texts but I thought they were a legend."

"Many legends are based on truth," said Remus quietly.

"Sure thing," the baroness said, pulling her robe tighter. She made her way to her sleeping room and her cozy pod, leaving Remus wondering if he should stay or go.

"I heard the baroness talking about exploring," said Loanmouth the baker. "People are always talking about her and getting it wrong. I don't think one should speculate," said Rugger.

"Well, I think she is gorgeous, but if she wants to destroy herself and everyone else in the process of proving a point, then she should be locked up," said O'Dowd the chemist.

"She might have a point," said Loanmouth. "What if the detectorists tested the above? They might find it safe and we can expand in the daylight," he continued.

"Loanmouth, Loanmouth everyone knows you would melt in the sun then turn into a dry husk," said O'Dowd.

"I don't think we know what happens to human skin in the above," said Rugger. "Best not speculate, like I said."

"Well mate, I am going to help her. I am going to volunteer to give her a hand," said O'Dowd.

Everyone looked at him quizzically. "Then make sure she does not succeed."

That evening in the feeding hall the Castle Rock survivors gathered to eat. People filed into the chamber with their spare water in plastic jars. The amount of water returned defined the size of the meal provided. The baroness could eat as well as she wanted but chose to provide food for the needy. This was a time when the collective protection was switched on and respirators were removed. Many did not like this, preferring the feel of rubber even on their faces. They tended to shave their heads and wear rubber skullcaps. They were androgynous and it was difficult to define their gender. The baroness was very clear about her femininity and when unmasked sat with the norm of feminine citizens.

Loanmouth, the baker, served pasta and soup to the line. He stood just over the baroness and managed to drop a note right in front of her. She quietly slammed her hand over the note and was not observed. Looking up, her ash blond hair glinting under the artificial light, she smiled and said,

"Have a good evening Master Baker." Loanmouth's heart raced.

"I will. Thank you, your dame-ness."

The collective survivors sang 'Amazing Grace' and listened to the latest news texts. 100 People had died of plague. They apparently did not inspect their respirators regularly. Twenty people were rewarded for respirator repair and maintenance. There is a pattern to all these broadcasts thought the baroness. It is all too similar day in day out, she thought. The baroness suspected the news guru was recycling the same news. There was only so much you could say about living underground. After reporting a rat infestation here and a pox breakout there, what was left?

Back in her apartment, the baroness threw the pack on the white table. She looked at the note. It said "Help is at hand". Strange thing to do, she thought. She gathered together her treasures, the items she could carry that she would miss too much to leave behind. There was a silver mirror and a matching hairbrush, and a collection of rings, as well as a small badge for an underwater swimming club from ancient Europe. She included a spare set of respirator lenses plus a tinted set to wear over her regular lenses.

There was an unexpected knock on her door. Pressing the reception light switch she could see it was Remus.

"Baroness, are we going today?"

"Sorry Remus, I will not know until later." She looked at the radio transmitter in the middle of the white table. "I need to conserve electricity in the battery. I will switch it on tonight when the radio waves travel further and hope to speak to the Angolans. I am so glad English is the language of the Aether," she thought out loud.

126

"Angolans - who would have thought the jewel in the crown of Africa was reality and not a myth."

Remus looked at her longingly but accepted her dismissal.

"OK Baroness, Ma'am. See you tomorrow forenoon."

"Yes, yes, see you Remus."

She watched him disappear down the corridor then closed the door. Removing her respirator as she sat down, she involuntarily smoothed her hair while she studied the radio set. Switching on the device it glowed green and came to life. She turned down the volume and, speaking into it, pressed the speak button. "Hello AUGUSTO, this is the baroness." It was a long moment before she heard the reply then the small speaker burst into life

"Hello Baroness, this is Imperial Angolan Airship THE AUGUSTO. We copy your transmission. Acknowledge. Over."

She replied "Hello AUGUSTO. My battery has limited life. Can you help me?" She waited and waited.

"Hello Baroness. Affirmative, this we can do. Be at the top of Castle Rock Colorado at eleven hundred hours tomorrow ready for rescue. Due to weight restrictions we cannot take anyone else this time as we have not victuals and fuel for such a diversion. Only one passenger is possible. The Captain looks forward to welcoming you on board and fully debriefing you on the predicament of survivors in the USA. Do you copy?"

"Yes, I copy," she said, her mind racing.

"Roger. This is THE AUGUSTO. Be seeing you, out."

Switching off the radio, she placed it with the spare battery in her belt order. The baroness removed her clothing slowly, each article a thought about the past, present, and future. She raised the periscope and caressed the brass, then headed to her shower room. Nothing for years then contact over the Aether, over the airwaves with technology surviving from a time before the catastrophe. The warm water felt comforting on her skin. After the dryers did their work she slipped into her sleeping pod and slept a dreamless sleep.

The baroness woke and quickly dressed. She made her way to her door thinking she would get an early breakfast then get on with her preparations. The door was locked and the magister and Remus stood on the other side. "You can't go Baroness!" Remus shouted. She felt her heartbeat rise and she panicked.

"No, Remus, open this door now."

"Sorry, Baroness, no can do," said the magister. "You are guilty of exploring."

"Wait!" she shouted. She grabbed the helmet with the sod of grass and held it to the porthole window of her door. "Look what I found. The Earth is restoring. This is real green grass."

"You are tricking us with green painted lies," the Magister spat through his respirator. The baroness stared out of the porthole looking wide-eyed when she heard a voice in her apartment, from behind her

"Lady, this is your escape route." She looked round and there was Loanmouth the baker.

"Well, I wanted to win a bet with O'Dowd, so if I help you, then I win. My family knows all of the secret passages and your stairway is here. I will deal with the magister and Remus. You go now and send the Angolans back to help us."

"You see everything I do in my apartment?"

"Of course not, not everything," he said. *Sorry. I lied*, he thought.

"This way, Lady, and goodbye." She looked at the wall where a doorway had appeared. The baroness kissed Loanmouth and he blushed.

"Away with you, Lady, and Godspeed."

She packed the parcel of grass into a tiny plas-glass vivarium, then into her backpack, and ran from her quarters up the spiral staircase, adjusting her best bird-beak respirator as she went. Stopping to hoist her long white skirt and tuck it into her black leather belt, she bounded up the stairs and came to a door high up in the rock. After checking her respirator seals, she pulled her long rubber gloves all the way up her arms. She tied the seals tight with their rubberized cord and checked the integrity of the black latex catsuit that she wore under her frilly white dress. This was it.

It took some effort to fit her family keys, usually kept on a chain around her neck, into the locks and pull back the latches. As expected, there was an airlock. A single porthole lit the scene. Sealing the door to her previous existence behind her, she turned to face the final door to the outside and the unknown. Through the window, she could see the dark shape of the Imperial Angolan Airship with its red and black markings and single gold crown. It was magnificent. She pulled the final X, Y and Z latches of the outer door but they were solid.

"Oh my God," she raged in pure frustration. To calm herself she thought of the four cornerstones of survival; Detection, Self protection, Collective protection and Decontamination. *We shall detect. We protect ourselves as the one and the all. We shall be clean and pure.*

She slammed the club hammer from her belt order onto the X latch and freed it. Smashing the Y and Z latches the door swung wide, creaking on its encrusted hinges. The airship was heading her way. The Angolans had heard her transmission. They had sent a vessel thousands of miles into contaminated America and now they were signaling with a heliograph. The baroness pulled a small hand mirror from her pack and flashed the reflected light of the setting sun in the direction of the dark lozenge shape. It adjusted course and lost height. It seemed to grow as it approached closer and closer, its nose pointing at the rock. The baroness scanned the landing area; glad it was clear of debris. There was the cluster of sensors of her periscope system, but they were no obstruction to this behemoth of the skies.

The baroness had never seen a real airship before. There was a massive A39 on the side. Open mouthed under her respirator, she breathed deeply and hoped her canister would hold out in the upper world. Then she could make out the sight of men working the gondola that was mounted under the envelope of lifting gas. They were smart black men all in blue-grey uniforms. On the flight deck she caught the glint of gold from the Captain's uniform. The noise of the fans was becoming louder.

It swooped down and hovered in front of her.

"Get on board quickly Madam, we cannot stay long. Get on board here Madam." The deep voice of the captain echoed over Castle Rock and the baroness ran to the ramp that had been lowered by the main gondola and suddenly she was on board and in a room with men wearing protective gear and respirators. They pulled her in and sprayed her down with foamy water.

She laughed and rubbed her hands together. "Wonderful!" she shouted "Wonderful!"

The sergeant felt himself being shaken. "Wake up, wake up Sarge."

"No. No. No. You can't stop this now, I am mid-story. What happens to the baroness? What?"

The sergeant looked up at the faces surrounding him in the Den and then said;

"I was snoring, right?"

"Yes," they all said as one. The dark lady twirled her black parasol and smiled.

"Sorry. I had better head home," he said.

As he went home on the steam train, he pulled his notebook out and scribbled down all he could recall. The baroness is special. She would return. He knew she would return.

Steve Moore is a member of the Steampunk Empire's Scribbler's Den and lives in London, United Kingdom. This flash fiction story connects with his first novel ROYAL AMERICA available on kindle from Amazon. Steve is a member of Bellack Productions a collective of UK writers looking for other ways to get their message to the public.

His website is www.royal-america.co.uk
Please dip in.

WHEN THE TOMB BREAKS

WILLIAM J. JACKSON

"YOU DON'T SAY? THE GUILD of Honor, here in my den?" the innkeeper scratched a beard pure white. Mister Kestrel had never had such unique company here in Philadelphia's Brothers Den.

"Sir," Aerie of Emerald sang, "you have near half of us. Hopefully enough to perform the deed." She represented the third of four paranormal sisters, uncanny women whose names graced many a scholarly dissertation. Tall and spindling with caramel skin, sweeping jade eyes and an overabundance of blue-green hair tied into a ponytail that arched up and away before trailing down to the peanut shell covered floor. Her voice shrilled as the pitch of bird calls.

Mister Kestrel noted her open-toed sandals and acute toenails, odd amenities to display on a brisk late September morning. Her sleeveless leather corset with dark green swatches, green feathers draped back over the shoulders and long, three-piece skirt of black and emerald meant to him the lady was aptly labeled. Oval goggles of bright brass tinted sea green sat atop her head. They in turn supported a tiny song sparrow, one unperturbed by human surroundings.

The Guild was known as much for its eccentricities as it was for saving the country, and the world, a score and seven times.

A regular to the Den in a relaxing red chair chimed into the discussion. "Glad you all came here, what with these pinheads moving into Pennsylvania, gumming up the works!"

Derogatory term aside, the paranormals he spoke of were the loathsome Catalog Couple. Years earlier, when the element negatrite was uncovered in Railroad City, Missouri, its radiating waves created random powers, 'talents', in many living things. People used these talents for many purposes. For the Guild, it came down to righting wrongs, proper civil discourse. But not everyone viewed light from the same angle. To many it meant…

"Vandalism!" Mister Kestrel finally let it out, to such a degree of excitement his Stockwell and Company goggles tilted to the right of his tweed cap. "That young man and his much older mistress blew away my brand new Automatic Engine! Sheffield installed it by the river three weeks ago and now…!"

"Mister Kestrel," the pronounced Serbian accent of Ahaziah Gujic (called the Horseman by many, though he disliked it) laid out words accompanied by a tinge of Western drawl, a unique American fusion. Salt and pepper hair were all that stood out on this average cowboy, that and a filthy duster. "We've tangled with these two—"

"One time too many!" Aerie's younger sister, the Crimson Aerial, cut in between Gujic's speech and her smacking on paraffin wax gum. "Shoulda shot 'em down back in Columbus." She sucked her teeth. Tall and brown like her sibling but shaped like an hourglass, Aerial's eyes were as crimson as her identical dress. She wore heavy steel-tipped boots, several leather belts and two sword-guns gleaming in silver, each one emblazoned with the name *Pretty*. Out of her back and elbows sprang dark iron rods that tapered to hollow points at their ends, rising slightly whenever she spoke. Kestrel could but guess.

Are they a part of…her body? he wondered, afraid to ask. *Are the rumors true?*

Aerie of Emerald converted from astute calm to distress. "Bite your tongue. You are speaking to your elder."

"Ah'm grown." Crimson Aerial's southern lilt, aside from her abruptness, further separated her from her older sister.

Kestrel, a father in his own right, knew when to cut into a sibling war. "Yes, well, might I show you the engine out back, and where I believe the vandals went?"

Without another word, Mister Kestrel marched to the back of his Den, beyond the sitting room with its cozy warmth, gargantuan fireplace and gabbing artisans from the far corners of the globe. This establishment existed in Philadelphia since the first Mister Kestrel arrived with William Penn himself, a resting post for weary travels. In the last twenty years, the current keeper, a connoisseur of art and literature, managed to attract to his inn artisans more accustomed to existence on the fringes of modern attachment. From day to night, the Den hosted writers talking to themselves aloud, artists offering unique visions of the local streets and forming masterpieces from the Den's shrubbery. Edwin Seer, the Guild's paternal figure, visited the Brothers Den five times during trips to the East, even bestowing upon Kestrel his favored pair of goggles. This was where the Grecian Empress wrote the final chapters of *The Colloquial Vapor Tyrant*, where Canadian and British adventurers used Stockwellian equations to prove (so they said) that parallel temporalities existed along variant universal harmonics. A site of legend shook hands this day with its modern day confederates.

He led the troupe of five, three women, two men, out a sturdy door and into a garden still verdant. Bushes handcrafted into a line of circus animals performed a paralytic parade along the brick pathway. The air, even this late in the season, swarmed with the movements of brown Woodcocks and Northern Flickers. The bright day rejuvenated their spirits, until the clanging, clattering rust beast Kestrel pointed to as the Engine bleated a song to ravish the eardrums.

Built like a water tower on a tall frame of grizzled iron, the Stockwell Automatic Engine was a steam-powered dynamo, a self-sustaining boiler lapping up water from the passing canal

Stockwell and Company dug to feed from the bucolic Schuylkill River. The boiler, a titanic cylinder of steel hosting a parasol roof and five lines of lead pipes, rocked side to side, crying as a woman in the throes of labor. Had the Brothers Den been directly in the city's bustling center, no doubt quite the fuss would be made about Kestrel's clamorous contraption.

"My cold lamps won't function now! Neither will the Autonomous Tractor!" He hollered over the din, barely heard by his guests. "My Old World clientele are eating up the fireplace, but American businessmen! Feh! New technology, or nothing! I'm losing prime business, and all for not renting a room to criminals!"

The previous evening the illustrious Catalog Couple, bedecked in the finest vestments from Paris, were on the run, as some say. Chased out of Tennessee by the Guild after a botched caper, they vanished in the moonless night. Keeping track of their movements via telegraph, telephone and word of mouth, the heroes heard of the Catalogs' attempts to seek lodging under the Den's soothing embrace. Accurate photographs of Mister and Mrs. Couple, reproduced and sent across the land by the Stockwell Emulation Agent, ruined their strategy. Mister Kestrel had (under pressure) invested in an Emulation Agent a month earlier. Those American businessmen…

"Do we build machinery on the go now?" Professor Flag Epsom asked, flooding the outdoors in a sarcastic tidal wave of Scottish bile. Steam from a mechanical box chugged around the wrinkled brown coat and over his battered top hat. Scruffy black eyes on a sour white face studied the surrounding Philadelphia countryside as if it bore every blight known to Man.

Mister Kestrel repressed his thrill to hear his idol speak at last. "Professor, please tell me you'll make use of your chronoscopic vision to see what transpired last night." He tried not to gleam like a schoolboy.

"Chronoscopic vision is not an official designation!" Epsom tapped his cane on the ground to expound his rage.

"Yes it is!" replied his comrades in unison. In truth, Epsom held an honorary status in the Guild, but his exploits in seeing the past earned him many a dime novel, even a penny dreadful in England (few in the States ever read *The Chronoscopic Man in the Salt Mines of Utter Dread*).

"Fine. Yew all call a man out of bed in the corpse dead of night to find two needles in God's haystack." Stepping to the engine on a false, spring-loaded left leg and the poodle-headed cane, Epsom lifted his right arm to touch the engine. The arm was also mechanical, a glossy thing of steel, of brass of springs and copper etchings. Epsom was a cranky lout before the mill accident that took his limbs. It seemed to Kestrel that being close to friends made the professor more bitter than bonny.

Per request, he let his talent unfurl. The black of his eyes widened until the whites of Epsom's eyes were snuffed out. He wandered the scene at a snail's pace. "Please Mister Kestrel, enlighten the Old Man and lasses to what happened while I take notes. Make it fast. Crimson Aerial gets restless."

"No I..." she said. "Well, true, but you say it so mean!"

"And never yew mind Mister Gujic. He cannae care less about this dilemma."

"I care." Gujic's placid face retained its canyon stillness as he folded his arms and appeared rather indifferent.

Kestrel reclined onto an iron bench. He waved for the ladies to take a seat next to him. Aerie and Crimson took up the offer, while the third heroine, Cosme, scoured the scene. Tiny, encompassed in black cloak and tights with copper wiring about the ankles and wrists, a black veil and matching lipstick on pouty lips. Mountainous lemon curls of hair filled the cloak's hood as Cosme gazed with huge eyes at the cemetery across the Schuylkill.

"Très romantique..."

The western outskirts of the City of Brotherly Love were truly a sight for sore eyes. Skyborne serpents of smoke slithered out of the city's thousand chimneys, a jungle of brick and stone hovels amidst a forest of flora. The sky, near white and cloudless, revealed Philadelphia to be a regal entity, a machination of moving parts. Trains as arteries, steam as blood, cells of people, black dots along capillary roadways. But the cemetery, artistic and green and graceful, took Cosme's breath away.

Kestrel grinned, an eggshell smile, wide as daybreak. "You, eh, fancy Laurel Hill?"

"*Oui, monsieur!* What other place is more entrancing to the heart than one so pretty, so forlorn."

Sisters Aerie and Crimson offered awkward smiles. Many do not look lovingly on homes for the dead.

Mister Kestrel pointed across the shining river. "I'm glad you approve, Miss Cosme, for that is where the Catalog Couple have been corralled. Men from the Army came here, quick as rabbits, at my summons. They've cordoned off the north, east and south. However, due to the reputations of the paranormal establishment—"

Gujic snorted. "They're too afraid to go in and get them! Typical." He spat on the grass, ignoring a perfectly good brass spittoon nearby.

"It's been several hours," Kestrel advised, "and I'd be sure as sunshine those vandals must be set on edge! Perhaps you'd best take care of them before they get desperate, while I figure out how to buy a new engine."

"Worry not about your engine, we have it coming along," said Aerie of Emerald. "Mister Gujic, might I fly you over to the other side, while my sister escorts Professor Epsom?"

"Why do I have to—?" Crimson Aerial moaned, but the hand of Emerald stayed her little sister's tongue.

Cosme, bereft of a flying partner, had other ideas. "I suppose it is time I tried out *Monsieur* Stockwell's idea, since the water is calm, *oui*?"

"Now?" half the party asked.

Cosme answered in her actions, backing away from the river, all the way, until she rested her tiny hands on the wall of Brothers Den.

Aerie of Emerald let loose her luscious hair, strands of broad follicles more akin to bird feathers, brilliant in the sunlight. At a glance, their reach was more than five times Aerie's own size, a visual feast of paranormal talent. The hair lifted in gentle strokes on its own, while Aerie took Gujic by the hands. In one rapid, downward motion, the mass of hair propelled the duo into the sky, creating an exhilarating breeze in the garden.

Crimson Aerial offered her hands reluctantly to the professor. The rods from her back and elbows began to spew steam, hot, whirring vapors. Her heels lifted from off the ground.

"Let's go, Professor. This will be easy, over in a minute."

"Lass, with a frame like yours clutching this old kettle to your bosom, there's no way this will be easy. On your back, or close up, 'tis a scandalous affair."

Ruby red goggles came down. Business superseded irritation. She let steam vent out at full force from the rods, cyclone pools of power, rocketing her forward. On the move over and up, she snatched Epsom from the ground before he could utter another complaint.

And Mister Kestrel? He gripped the bench, white knuckles and all. For a moment, he thought his eyes would melt for having seen what before only newspapers could describe. No words proved good enough for the real thing.

It was then, as the others arced over the Schuylkill (Crimson's rocket faster than Aerie's butterfly-esque flaps), that Kestrel recalled small Cosme, still against the wall. He saw she had changed, blue eyes were navy blue now, skin tight and shiny as polished porcelain. Thin ceramic tiles beneath her feet began to crack. He remembered a line from *Petite Cosme against the Blue Velvet Raiders* by Rail House Books:

"...for she attained, by the glow of negatrite, mastery over her cellular density. One minute, Cosme might be light as a feather. The next, as heavy as many ingots of lead."

He gazed across the Schuylkill River, and realized what feat the young lady was soon to experiment.

"Are you, concentrating on what you're about to do?"

The newfound heavy echo of her voice made Kestrel flinch. *"Non, monsieur.* I am imagining what the Couple's faces will look like, just before I punch them both *stupide!"*

"I cannot tolerate living like this, Cyril!" Veronica screeched. By now, surrounded by the Army, gawking reporters and suicidal children creeping behind Laurel Hill Cemetery's famed funerary statues had unnerved the veteran criminal. Already, Veronica Catalog (Veronica Vance of Jefferson, Missouri, alias Veronica Veil and the Countess of Cunning) had bitten three fingernails down to the second, pink layer of skin. Bleeding profusely, she licked away blood, her ginger curls bouncing around her head and mask of winged Derringers. The other hand, unbitten, pointed out onlookers in the distance by the stone entrance gate. "I was raised in finery, not the gutter!"

Cyril Catalog of Harrisburg, Pennsylvania (alias Cyril Roddenberry, Sye Balsam, Ned Talbert, Sidney Strayla, Benjamin Battle, Cyril Liryc and Chinese wagon cook Loo Fa) observed his chiseled features in the reflective surface of his steel gauntlet, brimming with rotating gun barrels. He admired his wonderful mane of black hair, upturned nose, the attractive mole on his left cheek, how his beady eyes squinted oh-so-right. Metallic wings, one broken (still a tad on the smoky side) rested on a backpack full of gears, of nozzles, of weaponry.

"Weren't we both, Sincerest Shade of Sultriness? Our parents' denial of our birthrights is how we came to be thieves, and the best at that." Cyril possessed a keen false British accent, one he used to woo many a woman from her purse, and Veronica into this life of debauchery. He admired himself whilst safely hiding behind a stone angel guarding a baby.

For the record, the Catalog Couple had been thieves long before they hunkered down in the Railroad City. Feeling the world owed them they hit banks, old ladies, loaded down mules and gold panners. They would have remained small time had they not been incognito in the Rail on the night negatrite exploded, silently, letting its iridescent waves infiltrate living things for miles. That night, they flipped through the pages of a worn Sears catalog. By morning, the couple uncovered some surprising features added to their repertoire...

"Adding matter to our bodies is a fine idea, save for the blasted heat!" Veronica continued her rampage, even setting off a few rounds of gunfire in the air. Nearby children went scattering for the hills. Birds, wiser than nosy humanity, had long fled the battlefield.

"Were we nearer to an armoury, Perfect Poison, I would readily add to our destructive capabilities."

"Then let us retire to one, so I might take on a more hellish garb!"

Cyril regarded his love with caution. Never had she appeared so vile - so unclean! Also, he discerned crow's feet around her eyes, dreadful signs of aging. He first offered comfort. "Very well, Angelic Arsenic. It isn't as if we haven't let off shot at soldiers and children before."

Barrels rotated along his back, fighting for space against the sturdy objectivity of a rusted Carver mortar. Thought loaded chambers to full with lead doom. As weapons readied, Cyril dwelled on his second, less sublime, decision.

After this, I simply must discard the hag to search out a new Mrs. Catalog.

A more perfect day for flying one could not ask for. Sadly, it fell on yet another day for war. Aerie of Emerald glided, barely flapping her winged locks, a serene vulture seeking the death reek of illegality. Ahaziah Gujic wasted the journey clutching his hat.

Landing better than a cat could manage, Aerie deposited Gujic behind a stately oak, he readying a rifle soon as feet touched earth. She went onward, landing at the height of the tree. From the ball of her exposed feet, curved talons extended to meet the ones growing from her toes. Emplaced to surveil, hair tying into a braid *sans* digital manipulation, she read the land.

A fiery rocket, blazing red, wilted leaves and kicked up a fuss along the ground. To this ground rolled (hard and luckless) Professor Epsom, tossing Gaelic complaints out between tumbles.

"Woman, kin yew nae drop a man in a manner befitting gentility!"

"Shut up, you fool!" Gujic hissed from across the cemetery path. "What if you give away our position?"

"Aye, position. For surely no one noticed a charioteering Negress and a giant pair of emerald wings blotting out the Sun!" Flag situated his ruffled brown coat, leaned the top hat forward, and quickly ducked behind a sturdy stone cross.

Crimson Aerial Rose over the treeline. "My, men complain a lot! As if you can't buy another hat and cane!" Bold as a hornet, she pressed on, *Pretty* One and Two at hand.

In an instant, Crimson found the uneven shape of Veronica Catalog, firing potshots at the cemetery's audience.

In a straight buzz, Crimson allowed her Pretties to shed weight, forty-five calibers at a time. Most found their way into the villainess' metallic shell, harmless pings alerting her to a rear assault.

"Crimson Aerial? Cyril!" Veronica watched Crimson speed by, straight, no maneuvers. She fired off a locust swarm of ammunition, a moment where possessing a Maxim attached to one's nervous system comes in handy. In between the barrage, "Her sister cut me the last time. I have a scar! A! Scar!"

Crimson Aerial's linear momentum made the counterattack against her all the more intensive. A chaotic line, lead shots, perforated her right side. Blood spray christened trees below. A few shots struck her metallic spine, bounding away, flat and useless. But enough did the deed to bring Aerial's course downward, a crashing human airship. A row of manicured bushes cushioned her impact while sacrificing their lives in an evergreen explosion.

Soldiers of the Regular Army raced into the hedge, rifles ready, uncertain what awaited them. Soil went up as the heroine pulled herself from a shallow ditch. She arose, stepping before a cluster of agitated gunmen.

"Whoa now!" She held her hands up, looking around to locate her missing babies. "Remember me?"

"No!"

Crimson bent over into a faltering sgrub. "There they are!" She posed with her guns, as if awaiting a photographer. "Remember now? This posture bring anything to mind?"

Rifles abutted her chest. One tapped a bullet wound, reminding Aerial she had been accosted. She grimaced.

"Guns down! Catalogs picked up an armed Negro, did they?"

"Ah'm Guild o' Honor! We fought the Sons o' Red Death together! Battle of Mobile?" She lowered the Pretties, clutched her injured, bleeding side. "Anyone?"

A soldier at the rear stepped ahead, pushing men's rifles downward. "I do. Easy, boys. She fought with us against the Indians, until they up and left us."

Crimson pouted. She felt lightheaded. "Well, y'all shoulda picked the...right...side..."

She fell into one man's arms as the sky caught fire. The Catalogs were unleashing their boundless fury.

"Ordnance is lighting up the air!" Aerie of Emerald screeched down to her comrades. "Even I can't see much!"

Gujic and Epsom advanced, one Graeco-Roman mausoleum at a time. Aerie ambulated across branches better than any squirrel, a perfect center of gravity being but one of many of her gifts.

"We'd have been better if my horse was here," Gujic peeked out to see one of their targets, Cyril Catalog, coming their way behind an armada of fire. Gujic fired two shots before the air thickened too much for anything but taking cover.

Flag took to running. "Yoo-hoo! Ugly ingrate! Yew could nae hit the broad side of the Queen's bustle!"

Cyril stopped his run to angle toward this new target. "Epsom! You kept the Wells Fargo cache from me!" He swallowed up Epsom's path in gnashing lead teeth. Like a bull shark, it chewed up land, devoured walkways, shattered stone monuments of beauty.

Who could endure such devastation?

A shining hand appeared from behind a family crypt after the violence.

"You're bloody welcome! Search your back, though!"

"What in the…"

Cyril caught the warning too late, the blow right on time.

Cosme let her density reach maximum as she ran across the yard. Heavier she was, yes, but also more powerful. Feet as small as a child's, but heavier than sledgehammers dug in, pushing the woman on steeled muscles to beyond steam engine speed. Wind at her back, perfect! The Schuylkill river met her fast. It was then she switched. Charcoal smoke spewed from her body, a frightening display making a watchful Mister Kestrel assume this heroine was fading away.

She surrendered the additional density for an even lighter frame. Boosted by this loss, energy transference, the blowing wind, the small mistress tiptoed at unfounded speed across the water's surface. Skipping, fumbling, delirious with glee, she persevered over the river, enjoying wind passing through her skin and organs.

She passed a steamboat ferrying passengers. Oh, the story they would later tell!

The first foot to touch land solidified, followed by the remainder of the body. The black smoke evaporated. Cosme leaned in, full tilt, full weight. She could see Cyril in the cemetery, turning to attack the professor. Losing a touch of speed, she cracked the walkway as she moved over it, making a straight line for the enemy.

"What in the..." Cyril saw too late. All her momentum centered into one tiny fist. It collided with Cyril Catalog's brass ladened chest, launching him back several yards. His body somersaulted back, last night's dinner forward.

Cosme never surrendered her speed until Cyrill hit the ground. Skidding to a halt, she began ripping guns from his back. Wrenching, tugging, she plucked off weapons while tapping his face with her foot.

"Stay down!"

Gujic, Epsom and Aerie closed in. Immediately Epsom understood the ramifications of their actions.

"Well, well, well!" Another fine kettle of fish we've cooked, yes!" Their current location had lost its passive decorum, its tranquil, manicured grace. Laurel Hill Cemetery seemed an ancient, severed diorama of the fall of Rome, bits and pieces, modern chaff unfit for display. Cyril's attack, and face first retreat, upturned flawless grass and cropped young trees.

"Are you taking our debt to the owner?" asked Aerie, crossing her arms, annoyed, gazing ahead for signs of her sibling.

"Aye, before someone less honest does! Shall we find Crimson Aerial before the lass gets herself entombed?"

Gujic advanced. "If Thunder had been here…"

"We know!" his allies roared. "This would be over by now!"

Cosme rested a heavy foot upon dizzy Cyril's sternum. " I have this dog. *Allons-y!*"

One remained. Three ventured on, where the weather revealed naught but a whirlwind of screams, hail of bullets.

Crimson Aerial stared indifferently at her fast clotting wounds. Her back was a mighty mess, one iron pipe bent. A minute earlier she took to the searing task of straightening it out by hand. No different than mending one's broken arm by shifting the parts together, she reached behind, tugged up and sideways. Now, spine flaring, neck stiff, she sat and watched the futile advance if the United States Regular Army into the cemetery.

It reminded her of the charge over the hill at the Battle of Dead Still; same foolish rush, identical results. Young men went in between crypts, never to walk out. She found the setting fitting. Pings and pops so close to city living sent citizens evacuating.

Veronica Catalog possessed one advantage in a fight. Utter, shrieking insanity. While most suppressed this volatile trait, she found it improved her aim, increasing the amount of spittle falling from otherwise lovely lips. She unleashed a Crimean War on cemetery grounds. Soldiers posed no threat. Armored by rotating iron shields, buffered now by spinning cavalry swords, Veronica strode the battlefield victorious, and very unladylike.

She took no notice of the uncountable number of birds darkening the sky. Or perhaps she did, as their feathery cloudmass multiplied her ire.

"The dilemma with madness is, one forgets to count."

"Who said that?" Mrs. Catalog screeched. The air, inundated by shooting, should block all other sound.

A smidgen of reason dawned. "Aerie? Talking through your avian cousins? Devolved savage!",

Then the cemetery was reduced to its most basic sum. Silence. Veronica Catalog ran clean out of shot. A terrible position to be in when one is a villainess surrounded by the law. And legions of birds.

"Eh...ah…" Veronica's eggshell armor over her mind quaked. Digging fingernails polished by gunmetal into her soft chin, she let out a succulent scream.

Right before the swarm of birds stampeded.

"One of our easier adventures," affirmed Aerie of Emerald.

"Mass destruction is termed 'easier' in your estimation?" Mister Kestrel observed. Grateful he was, but seeing raw power first hand brought a sincere reserve to his exhilaration.

The narrow dirt road to Brothers Den held swarms of people. The same runaway Philadelphians returned to complain about their ravaged garden by the river and gawk at the spectacle coming their way.

Cheering children scattered to make way for the horse pulling the new Stockwell Engine. Red Thunder, Horse of Horses, strode to the Den. Draft horse huge, red as roses, entire body pulsating circles of bass tones. Every hoofbeat created steady vibrations to tickle the bones of onlookers. Its mane was not hair, but waves of scarlet fury. Men said it was unkillable, more destructive than a dozen twisters, yet here it walked and stopped peaceful as daisies in a light breeze. They wondered how the Horseman could ride the beast.

"Hello, friend," Gujic approached his partner. "Good job. Good job. Sure did miss you in that beef. Mister Kestrel, you will be back in operation in no time."

Kestrel hesitated before touching the horse's neck. A pleasant reverberation entered him, righted old arthritic pangs. He laughed. "My, a day I have to tell to everyone who comes into the Den!"

Crimson Aerial, pained but defiant, and Cosme, smoky dense again, together lifted up the engine over their heads.

"How would you like it installed, sir?"

Mister Kestrel put his goggles to his eyes. "With all hands in! Shall we?"

Inside Brothers Den, genius minds looking out of the windows with fervor began putting pen to paper, and told the tale in a hundred ways.

William J. Jackson is a purveyor of alternate worlds, the Railroad City and beyond. His first novel, *An Unsubstantiated Chamber,* takes place in the years after this very tale. When not writing, Mr. Jackson lies in a coma, imagining next.

You can follow him on Twitter @railroadcity and on Facebook under author-williamjjackson.
Website: therailbaron.wordpress.com
Wattpad: @WilliamJJackson

ALL THAT GLITTERS

KAREN J CARLISLE

THE GROUND SHUDDERED. A roar thundered from the depths of the mine. Metal scraped. Gears ground.

Puffs of grey smoke rolled out of the tunnel's entrance. Streaks of black stained the clouds. The greasy smell of oil filled Alice's nostrils.

The ground shuddered again. A blast of sulphur stung Alice's eyes. Tears rolled down her cheek.

She sniffed at the air. *Black powder?*

Alice scanned the buildings along the edge of the camp – the tool shack, generator shed.

Empty.

The heavy spanner slipped from her hand and clattered onto the transport rail at her feet. She slammed the lid onto the Gas Extractor.

"Soo Lin?"

The earth moaned.

Dry air caught in the back of Alice's throat. Her lungs convulsed, expelling debris.

"Get out. Now!" She straddled the narrow rail line, grabbed the switch handle and peered into the swelling mass of smoke.

Another rumble bellowed out of the tunnel.

Where are you?

The handle writhed in Alice's hand. She braced her body and fought to calm the gyrations. Her elbow tendons twinged.

The rail vibrated through her boots.

Alice scrutinised the smoke. Shadows hissed and clacked amongst the plumes. The vibrations intensified. Shadows coalesced. A string of white smoke pierced the gloom. A petite woman, in tan overalls, stood on a box-like railcar, wrestling with the vehicle's lever. She wrenched it backwards, almost throwing herself to the floor.

"It's about time," said Alice.

Soo Lin frowned. "You duck."

"I'm a what?"

The railcar shuddered to a stop. Soo Lin jumped off the railcar and somersaulted behind the generator shed. Long dark braids whipped against her back as she landed silently.

Alice snatched up her spanner and turned to face the tunnel.

"What have you done?"

"Not me," replied Soo Lin. "A dragon."

"A what?"

"I throw huo yao. Dragon gone." Her brilliant white grin peeked out from under an enormous pair of blackened goggles.

Alice scanned the railcar. It was empty.

"Not the whole box?" she asked.

"If ignore dragon he will eat you," she replied.

"Always a proverb," said Alice.

Soo Lin shrugged.

"There are no dragons in Humbug Scrub, Soo Lin. Snakes, kangaroos, Howlers yes – but nothing as big as a dragon. They just don't exist."

"It have big shiny eyes. It growl. It breathe smoke. What *you* call it?"

A roar thundered out of the tunnel.

"Down!" yelled Soo Lin. She grabbed Alice's trousers and yanked her behind the shed.

A low rumble shook the guts of the mine.

Alice slipped the goggles over her eyes and peered around the edge of the shed toward the tunnel. The sound grew louder, creeping closer to the surface, and cracked through the entrance with a deafening boom.

Alice dodged back behind the wall of the shed, hoping it would hold under the concussive force.

Clods of earth rained on her head. The smell of sulphur caught at the back of her throat. She glanced at Soo Lin and covered her ears.

"What have you done?" asked Alice.

Soo Lin's eyes widened. Her gaze dropped to the ground.

Alice adjusted her goggles and squinted in the direction of the mine.

Choking clouds of brimstone belched from the tunnel and rolled along the floor in a cumulous wave. Filter masks jiggled on the shed wall, as if to vex her. Alice spluttered and snatched one from its hook.

"Bloody hell." The curse crackled in Alice's throat. Her eyes watered. "My mine!" She wiped the moisture from her nose and eyed Soo Lin.

Soo Lin remained crouched behind the shed, her eyes still fixed on the ground. She shook the dirt from one of her braids, coiled it behind one ear and pinned it in place. Her fingers untangled the other braid, shook it and coiled it behind the other ear, as she stood slowly.

"Are you all right?" asked Alice.

Soo Lin swallowed and nodded.

"Come on, fire up the Gas Extractor. We need to check the damage." Alice shook out the mask and surveyed the area.

Soo Lin remained behind the shed.

"Soo Lin?"

There was no answer.

Alice turned to face her friend. Soo Lin stood, staring at her feet, her shoulders slumped.

"Soo Lin, please look at me."

Soo Lin dragged her gaze up and locked her attention on Alice's chin. The lines around Soo Lin's eyes deepened, creating crevices that crept along her forehead. Tears welled up along her eyelids. Her mouth crinkled. Alice had not seen Soo Lin this upset since she first met her, after her husband had absconded to the gold fields.

A wave of dread flooded over Alice's body.

"Are you injured?" Her heart sank into her stomach. "Is there something you're not telling me?"

Soo Lin shook her head and sniffed. Her gaze fell back to her feet.

"Sorry. I panic. It is my fault. I will pay –" Soo Lin's voice was muffled. She reached into her pocket.

Not injured. Alice's muscles relaxed. Her heart slowed. *Thank God.*

They shared a common bond. Alice's wretched husband had abandoned her, lured by easier pickings in New South Wales. Soo Lin helped her run his neglected mine. They made a formidable team; with Alice's engineering skills and Soo Lin's knowledge of explosives, they had delved beyond the shallow copper deposit.

There's a wealth of gold down here – if we could only catch our thief. Alice straightened her shoulders and took a deep breath. Her friend was worth more than broken beams or a collapsed mine. Alice turned to Soo Lin. She spoke slowly.

"Don't worry. Accidents happen." She placed her hand on Soo Lin's shoulder. "Come on; let's go find your dragon."

Alice rubbed her ear, still feeling the effect of the explosion. She pulled her mask over her face and strode into the smoke-filled tunnel. The swirling cloud obscured her vision. Her boot scraped the metal rail. She reached out her arm to steady herself, groping the air until her fingers scraped against compacted earth.

A loud clank of metal gears echoed down the tunnel behind her. Soo Lin cursed in Cantonese. The Gas Extractor responded with a long hiss and chugged into life.

A gentle breeze dragged smoke past Alice's cheek toward the tunnel entrance. She ran her fingers along the wall as she inched further into the tunnel.

Footsteps padded up behind her. An eerie smudge of yellow light bobbed along the tunnel. Her muscles tensed.

A gas lamp? Fire! What if it set off another explosion?

Dark patches of clean air formed in the tunnel.

"Is the gas lamp safe?" Alice asked.

Soo Lin nodded.

"No huo yao." She sniffed the air. "Gas gone. Safe now."

Small wisps of smoke curled around Alice's ankles, as she sucked filtered air through her mask. Soo Lin's father had taught his daughter everything he knew about fireworks and explosives. She wouldn't risk their safety.

Alice's muscles relaxed.

Alice and Soo Lin trudged down the tunnel, following the vein of copper as it curved down to the gold deposits. Alice rounded a corner, and almost slammed into the pile of boulders. Debris blocked the tunnel, spilling over the twisted rail.

"Bloody hell!"

"Perhaps we find way through?" Soo Lin smiled weakly, picked out a few smaller rocks and tossed them to the ground.

Alice nodded. She scrabbled up the debris to reach the smaller rocks. She pushed, pulled and wriggled them. They wouldn't budge. She leaned toward the edge of the rubble and tested the rocks there. Warm air trickled over her hand.

Alice chuckled. She wriggled her fingers.

"There's air coming through a crack here. Perhaps the explosion breached the mine?" she said.

"Another way into tunnel?" replied Soo Lin.

Alice nodded. "We need to go rabbiting."

"Rabbiting?" asked Soo Lin.

"We're looking for a very large rabbit hole," replied Alice.

Shadows crept across their camp. Alice glanced upward. Grey clouds crept in from the south.

A faint clop ground on the loose stones.

"Looks like rain," said a voice.

Hot breath rushed over Alice's neck. A horse whinnied near her ear. She recoiled from the sound. She turned to see a stout, well-dressed man atop a thoroughbred horse. He tipped his hat in Alice's direction.

"Good afternoon, Mrs Drake." He wheeled the horse, turning his back on Soo Lin.

"Is it, Mr Roach? It's not that grand from where I stand. I'm delighted to hear you are having a more fortunate one."

Soo Lin lifted her finger to her lips and shook her head. Alice dusted off her trousers and cleared her throat.

"And to what do I owe the pleasure of your company?" asked Alice.

"I saw the smoke. I thought I would check my neighbour was safe," He tapped his hat back in place.

"How thoughtful of you," said Alice.

"My offer for the mine still stands." He glanced back to the smoking tunnel, put his gloved hand to his mouth and coughed. "Unless there is extensive damage, of course."

"It's nothing serious," said Alice.

"I worry for you, Mrs Drake." The reins fell from his hands as he gestured toward the surrounding trees. "All alone in the bush."

"I'm not alone."

"No one to protect you from the natives." He leaned forward in his saddle. "When will you come to your senses? A mine this size cannot be run by a woman. You need men to work it."

"I have Soo Lin."

Roach eyed Alice and wrinkled his nose.

"No wonder your mine has been unproductive."

"Only because someone is stealing our gold."

"Theft? That's a serious accusation, Mrs Drake." Roach raised an eyebrow. "I hope you have proof to back up your story."

Proof?

Alice's eyes narrowed. She straightened her shoulders and glanced at Soo Lin.

Soo Lin shook her head. She raised her hands, curled her fingers and made hopping movements, like a rabbit. Alice bit the corner of her lip, trying not to smile.

"Why bother yourself with such an ill-fated venture when you could afford to take a house in town, relax and concentrate on more…" He eyed her dusty clothing and raised an eyebrow. "… Lady-like pursuits. I'm going to Steventon: If there's anything you need…"

Alice grabbed the reins and handed them to Roach.

"Thank you for the offer," she replied, as she slapped the horse's neck. Its muscles twitched. "We need no assistance."

"As you wish, Mrs Drake." Roach drove his heel into the horse's flanks.

Alice watched the horse trot out of sight. Soo Lin removed her goggles and squinted in their wake, her eyes two pale circles ringed with soot and dust.

"With money, you are dragon," said Soo Lin.

"With too much money, you're a worm," added Alice.

Soo Lin laughed. "You do listen."

Alice nodded and scanned the sky. "Looks like it will rain," she said

Soo Lin plucked up the lamp. "After rabbiting, we find proof."

Twigs snapped under Alice's feet. Branches snagged her blouse and scratched her arms, as she trekked through the dense scrub. She glanced behind her. Soo Lin danced her way through the undergrowth, avoiding entanglements.

Wooden talons scraped Alice's trousers. The branches snapped. The smell of eucalyptus filled the air. Alice breathed in the fresh aroma; the sweet, pungent smell filled her nostrils. She glanced up at the sky. The light was fading. Dark clouds hovered close to the hilltop.

"We should have fetched the oilskins," said Alice.

A chilled breeze washed over her face. A blob of rain fell onto her arm. Another plopped onto her eyelash and rolled into her eye.

Alice's foot rolled on the rocky ground. She rubbed her eye and blinked her vision clear. A wide crack snaked along the ground toward a shadowed clearing further down the gully.

"Our rabbit hole?" asked Soo Lin.

Alice scrambled to her feet and searched the scrub. She picked her way over the uneven ground along the crack. Soo Lin padded close behind.

"I would have expected a lot more debris with an explosion of that size," said Alice.

Alice stepped over a thick fallen branch. The ground collapsed under her weight. She sank into the damp, dark earth.

Cold sludge oozed into Alice's mouth and between her fingers. Dirt trickled down her collar. Splashes encircled her in the dark. Her ankle throbbed.

Alice opened her eyes. The lamp lay on the ground a few feet away, its glass cracked.

Soo Lin picked up the lamp and examined the casing. She shook the lamp, twiddled the knob and lit the wick. A glimmer of light emanated from the mantle, sputtered then slowly filled the cavern with its comforting glow.

Pale yellow mud clung to Soo Lin's skin and weighed down her overalls. She rushed toward Alice. Thud, squelch. Frowning, she shook her foot; one slipper drenched.

Alice pushed herself up to her knees and spat out the offending mud. The air was cold and damp. There was a smell, like…

She blew flecks of dirt from her nose.

Like coal.

She surveyed the cavern. Dust danced in the faint shafts of light streaming from the jagged maw in the earth above their heads. Drips of rain thudded on the exposed roots and plopped to the ground next to Alice. Water seeped from a crack in the nearby wall and bled into puddles. Small wavelets rippled and glistened in the lamp light. The cylindrical burrow curved away into the darkness away from the mine.

"That's one big rabbit hole." Alice ran her hand along the walls. A deep furrow spiralled along its length. Was this the work of Soo Lin's dragon? *Not possible.* The surface was too regular. "I think your dragon went that way," she said.

Alice and Soo Lin followed the burrow further away from the mine into the darkness, towards the dragon's den.

The light from the lamp swung back and forth across the burrow.

Left, right. Alice followed its movement with her head.

Left. Right. It helped her to forget her aching feet.

Left. Right.

Her chin itched. She rubbed her face. Dry mud crumbled over her hand. *How much farther?*

The light jiggled. Alice shook her head. Her ankle twinged.

"Light ahead," whispered Soo Lin.

"Turn off the lantern."

Alice drifted into the shadows near the wall and crept toward the opening ahead. Soo Lin followed in the dark. The burrow opened onto a cleared area of bush. Alice slipped behind a mound of earth to survey the clearing.

Leaves rustled in the tall gums. Shadows flickered across the ground, skittered up and over tin-roofed buildings and along the netted fence near the gums.

Moonlight danced over scattered dirt-encrusted mechanicals. A sharp-angled leviathan shrouded in canvas stood near a long shed, not far from the burrow. A wooden platform rose from the middle of the clearing. A long metal shaft ran down the centre of the contraption, pierced a maze of cogs and gears, and sank into a deep shadow in the ground below. Nothing moved.

On the far side of the encampment, a track wound down the gully back toward the road. Half way up the hill a pale homestead glowed in the moonlight. The windows were dark.

"It's Roach's mine," she whispered to Soo Lin. "Everyone's most likely down in Steventon whooping it up in the pub for the night."

Canvas slapped and tinked in the breeze. Alice eyed the covered giant.

"I wonder what's hidden under there?" She crept behind a nearby tree and motioned for Soo Lin to follow.

A faint crack echoed through the camp. Alice slammed her body against the trunk. Soo Lin rolled and landed next to her.

Who's there?

A melodic warble drifted down from the tree. They glanced up into the canopy. A small shadow flitted higher into the branches. It tilted its head back and sang again. Another warble replied from across the camp. Alice took a deep breath.

Bloody magpies. She chuckled and continued toward the canvas mound, peeking through a shed window as she inched past. Shadows of generator equipment were barely visible in the darkness.

Empty. Alice smiled. They were alone. She continued toward the canvased curiosity.

Several tarpaulins had been lashed together to cover the monstrosity. Alice grabbed a corner and peeked under the covering. A faint whiff of coal dust wafted upward. A domed portal stared blankly back at her.

"Soo Lin, bring the lamp." Alice peeled the canvas away from the bulk to reveal another domed portal on the opposite side, this one cracked.

Soo Lin held the lamp closer. A pointed, screw-like nose jutted from one end. The glass domes glistened and winked at them.

Shining eyes.

Soo Lin gasped.

"I think we've found your dragon," said Alice. "It's a mechanical digger." She pushed the canvas further up the hull.

Scorch marks blackened part of the casing on the far side. Soo Lin ran her fingers along the marks.

"Your work, I believe," said Alice.

Soo Lin nodded and smiled.

"I knew it was Roach," said Alice. "He's been using it to dig under the mine and steal the gold from under us. The cad!"

"Our proof," said Soo Lin.

Alice shook her head. "No, he could move it before the Constabulary arrive. We need more." She eyed the homestead on the hill. "And I know where to get it."

She pulled the tarpaulin back over the digger and headed up the track toward the homestead.

The house was dark. More importantly, it was empty.

Alice tiptoed down the hall, checking the rooms as she went until she found Roach's office. A carved oak desk dominated the room. Sturdy bookshelves flanked the window behind it. A small curio cabinet stood beside a leather couch on the other side.

Soo Lin scrutinized the bookshelves.

Alice marched to the desk and sank into the soft, padded leather of Roach's chair. Her eyes widened.

"I could get used to this," she whispered.

Alice scanned the desk: a carved ink set and blotter, a diary, a ledger and a large quartz crystal currently being used as a paperweight. She rummaged through the drawers. The bottom drawer wouldn't open. She leaned in closer. A small keyhole was hidden amongst the carvings. Alice eyed Soo Lin.

"You don't happen to have any more black powder, do you?" she asked, smiling.

Soo Lin placed the lamp on the desk and shook her head. Alice's smile slipped. Soo Lin grinned. She poked her finger into her bun, pulled out a pair of curved hairpins and presented them to Alice.

"Will these do?" asked Soo Lin.

She crouched in front of the drawer, plunged the hairpins into the keyhole and jiggled them. There was a satisfying click. She slipped the pins back into her bun and eased open the drawer.

"You're a wonder, Soo Lin." Alice scooped out the contents and laid them on the desk near the lamp. There were documents and papers, stuffed envelopes and...

She unfolded a large map, plopped the nugget on one corner and pressed the paper flat. *A survey map.* She traced her finger along the lines of the river, across the gully to...

"This is a survey map of our mine," hissed Alice. She folded the map and slapped it together.

Soo Lin frowned and handed her a letter.

Alice shoved the survey map inside her blouse and scanned the letter. It was an application for a mining license reallocation—

"For our mine." Alice crumpled the letter in her hand and shoved it in her pocket. "How dare he!"

"We have proof?" asked Soo Lin. "We go now?"

Soo Lin glanced out of the window. She grabbed Alice's arm and dropped to the floor, pulling Alice down with her.

"What—?"

Soo Lin thrust her hand over Alice's mouth and shook her head.

A beam of light shone through the window and ran across the wall. Alice held her breath.

Footsteps trudged toward the house. The light darted across the ceiling and ducked back out the window. The front step creaked.

Alice's arm snaked up the desk. She felt her way across the blotter, past the ledger. Her fingers curled around the quartz paperweight.

"Grab the lamp, Soo Lin. Get ready to run."

The next step squeaked. Alice jumped to her feet and hurled the quartz through the open window. It clattered across the stable's tin roof. The crunching steps retreated, sped across the yard toward the stable.

"Run!"

They dashed down the hall, jumped the steps and barrelled down the track into Roach's camp. Alice's ankle burned. She bit her lip and ran on, past the platform, past the digger, toward the generator shed.

Soo Lin dashed into the shed. The generator chugged. There was a clank. Soo Lin burst out of the door and launched herself towards the mouth of the burrow.

"A diversion?" asked Alice, as she ran past Soo Lin.

Soo Lin nodded and ran after her.

The shed whined. A shudder reverberated through the walls.

Boots thundered across the stones behind them. Shots cracked in their wake, echoing around the gully. The shed door slammed.

Alice ran down the burrow. Ran into the darkness. Back to their mine. Soo Lin's footsteps padded past her.

A soft voice laughed.

"In shallow holes, moles make fools of dragons."

Karen J Carlisle writes speculative fiction including: steampunk, Victorian mystery and fantasy. She was short-listed in Australian Literature Review's 2013 Murder/Mystery Short Story Competition and published her first novella, *Doctor Jack & Other Tales*, in 2015. Her short story, *Hunted*, is currently featured in the Adelaide Fringe exhibition, 'A Trail of Tales' (atrailoftales.com). She is currently working on the next instalment of *The Adventures of Viola Stewart* and a new steampunk adventure series, *The Department of Curiosities*.

Karen lives in Adelaide with her family and the ghost of her ancient Devon Rex cat.

She has always loved dark chocolate and rarely refuses a cup of tea.

Follow her on twitter: @kjcarlisle, or facebook:
facebook.com/KarenJCarlisle
Website: *www.karenjcarlisle.com*
Goodreads: *https://www.goodreads.com/KarenJCarlisle*

Yggdrasil's Triumphant Return

Alice E. Keyes

YGGDRASIL CLIMBED THE SIX STEPS from her bedchamber to the deck thinking it was her last morning to command her crew of two, Dogwood and Dahlia. Dogwood, aloft, unfurled the large sail in front of the balloon, taking advantage of the morning breeze.

"Homecomings are always a burden and a joy." Dahlia handed Yggdrasil a cup of morning broth. Yggdrasil never asked Dahlia about the broth because she didn't want to know the concoction's contents. It tasted floral and spicy and gave her energy while taking away the morning hunger pains. On the longest periods aloft, sometimes it was their only nutrition for days.

"Estimated arrival time, Dogwood?" Yggdrasil shouted at his dangling figure.

"Afternoon tea." After tending the sail, he went behind decks for his four hours of sleep.

Yggdrasil might be a goddess but she ran her aircraft, *Signy,* according to the old sailing vessels traditions. After the mission of one and half years, they now moved in a symbiotic rhythm existing on four hours of sleep per shift. The break from this routine occurred when they reached a town where their mission was to count and to helped magical beings.

A duty of gods and goddess was to take care, keep in line, and manage the magical world and its various creatures. When Måni devised this mission for Yggdrasil, to mostly remove her from his court, he didn't realize she'd relish the chance for an adventure. She'd tired of the day-to-day world of tea parties, lawn games, and evening balls.

Yggdrasil thought about all of those languid uneventful days of Måni court life. Today, the thing she desired most from the past was a bed that didn't sway.

Dahlia, spotting the castle, Zahra, called out, "Home off starboard bow."

Yggdrasil smiled at the site of the castle but then pouted seeing an elegantly set tea table with Nanna sitting and already sipping tea with a book held in her hand.

"That's not much of a greeting," said Dahlia.

Dogwood came from below decks. "Dogwood, you did send a telegram at Boothby saying we'd arrive at the castle in three days time?" Yggdrasil asked

"Yes, of course, I remember the clerk, her nimble fingers and ample..." Dogwood's stopped hands showed the size of the woman's chest. Yggdrasil and Dahlia, as usually, didn't pay attention to this since it was always the same remark made about any woman he encountered.

Angered by the tranquil scene below, Yggdrasil paced, deep in thought. "Harrumph, I would, at least, expect the castle's own Måni to be waiting tea for us though I was expecting a full blown party at our return." Yggdrasil walked the deck looking from the castle windows to Nanna. "We'll make a spectacular entrance at least. I want to land two feet from Nanna and the tea table. Let's put a ripple in the milk."

From this one command, the three of them controlled the airship in a measured magically hum. The milk might not have rippled but they did ruffle Nanna's hair and landed precisely at the commanded two feet from the tea table.

"Yggdrasil you're adept at making an entrance though why with only me to witness. Is it not enough, with the castle empty, that I had tea set for you and your weary traveling crew?" Nanna barely looked up from her book.

"Where are the Fates, the court, and Måni?"

"While you've been spying on our fellow magical companions, the Fates are working in Iceland on the science of prediction. Everyone else has left on some sort of mission."

Yggdrasil knew of Nanna's sole mission. "How's your egg?"

"Egg?" Dahlia asked after anchoring the *Signy*.

"Yes, Nanna has been taking care of a dormant Joro-Wyrm egg for the last couple of centuries."

"Wow, when will it hatch?" asked Dogwood stuffing a strawberry biscuit in his mouth.

"I said dormant. It just sits there."

Nanna sighed and slowly closed her book. "Not lately, It's glowing blue and 10 times its normal size. This is the first moment I've been away from it for the last five months. I used your homecoming as an excuse to breathe fresh air and get some sun on my pale face." She turned from Yggdrasil, faced the sun, and closed her eyes when she felt its warmth.

Yggdrasil moved so that she blocked Nanna's sun. "Five months without a ball or garden tea party? Surely, there's someone besides you to watch it."

Nanna remained seated with her eyes closed. "Haven't you been listening? Everyone is gone and I'm am left with a staff of three. We've closed down most of the castle."

Yggdrasil plunked down in the seat. Nanna didn't look like her vivacious self. Her skin was pale and pasty and instead of an immaculate and wrinkle free silk gown, she wore a blue cotton day dress with a dark stain down the front and dirt along the hem.

Yggdrasil poured herself a cup of tea and when she added a lump of sugar, Nanna stood. "Back to the egg. It's growing too rapidly and if it continues at this rate I fear it will be the Kolvandre dragon instead of the Frîlîki dragon we're hoping for."

"It's one of the last eggs from Joro-Wyrm dragon, right?" asked Dogwood. Nanna nodded, stood, and walked away.

"Then it's the last hope for a continuation of the dragons species," Dahlia put down her cup and went to Nanna's side. Dogwood followed. "Is the story true that if a Kolvandre dragon is born of Joro-Wyrm egg then the magic beings of the Earth will fade and man will be on its own."

Yggdrasil watched and listened as Nanna and her crew walked away.

Dogwood put his arm around Nanna and said, "You know, we encountered a lot of troubled magical creatures on our mission. We can help."

Yggdrasil choked on her sip of tea. Dogwood giving comfort? His advice when encountering a forlorn elf was rolling his eyes and mumbling something about getting a backbone.

Yggdrasil crumbled a biscuit in her hands, sighed, and followed too. Her crew was great at piloting the *Signy* but, as far as, analyzing and coming up with solutions for magical beings gone awry, they were woefully incapable. The last encounter with a minotaur proved it.

On the walk back to the castle, Yggdrasil bit her tongue several times to keep from yelling. She couldn't believe the solutions Dahlia and Dogwood babbled like the dragon egg had come down with a sniffle instead of spelling out doom and the end of magical beings. The story Dogwood mentioned was not a fairytale but a prediction from the three fates that Joro-Wyrm's last egg spelled either a new beginning for the magical Celtic world or its demise. Yggdrasil had read the full three-hundred scroll report that indicated it wouldn't be the end of her kind, the gods and goddesses. Once she discovered this bit, she gave the egg no further thought especially, when Nanna was handed the egg to be its sole keeper. Yggdrasil couldn't imagine such a boring mission.

Thoughts about the egg distracted her from the path they were taking within the castle. They didn't turn toward the narrow hallway where Nanna had kept the egg in a small dark room but entered the main den and in Yggdrasil's opinion the best room in the castle.

The room was dark and barely recognizable with curtains covering the windows from the floor to the ceiling. The bright yellow and gold murals could not be seen. The mustiness and dank feeling gave it a cave-like atmosphere. One dim light, sitting on a desk covered with scrolls and papers in the corner, was the only illumination.

"That's a horrid reek," said Dogwood in his typical overt manner.

Dahlia wrinkled her nose, "It smells of cat pee mixed with sulfur."

"Close," said Nanna.

Dogwood gagged. "What?"

In the far end fireplace sat a huge cauldron with glowing embers at the base. Nanna gestured toward it with one hand while the other hand caressed the egg's nose. "It's alright darling, they may be able to help, slow your process, calm your fire, my sweet one." Nanna took her hand off the egg and faced Dogwood and in a schooling tone informed him. "I'm simulating Joro-Wyrm's cave. Dr. Spublick, the last known expert on dragon eggs, had the recipe in his scroll on mothering your egg."

Dogwood wafted the scent toward his nose and said. "Mmm, it adds a nice piquet to the room."

Yggdrasil shook her head seeing that Dogwood was under Nanna's spell though it didn't take much for Dogwood to be under any female's spell.

Nanna started to hum a tune for a moment and walked over to the cauldron, "One of the scrolls described making the egg comfortable by increasing the humidity in the room but I haven't had the manpower to even attempt it. Dogwood, I want you to bring in wood, water, and man the fire. I have enough sulfur concoction to add for a while. So, for every gallon of water you add to the cauldron, add a cup of concoction." She started to hum again and walked toward the desk stacked with scrolls.

Dogwood scratched, stared, and didn't move. "Did she mean now?"

Dahlia stared at him for a moment. "Yes, of course now. The egg isn't going to cure itself." Dahlia went and stood by Nanna at the table ready for her instruction.

Yggdrasil, during this exchange, walked around the egg counting her steps. It took her three hundred and twenty steps to go around the egg. The last time she saw the egg, Nanna had cradled it in her arms. Once a year, Nanna would take it to the Fates who determined if it should rest another year at the castle or if it should be moved. On this day, everyone in the castle liked to take a moment to see the egg.

Yggdrasil's studies about dragon eggs indicated that eight years were needed to incubate the egg to hatching size, not a mere six months. The situation might be dire. "When did everyone leave? Who has been reading my reports? Nanna this is so extremely odd for the castle to be empty."

Nanna was going through the pile of scrolls before her. She would open one then set it down and then go to another. After she set down the third one, she reached into her dress pocket and pulled out an ocular device, "You'll be interested in this one, Dahlia. Perhaps your knowledge will help make sense of the drawings"

"Nanna, answer me. Where has everyone gone?"

Nanna sighed, "I don't know. My only concern is the egg. The answer is probably in those correspondences." She waved at the area behind the desk of scrolls.

Yggdrasil went to stacks of varying sizes of envelopes. She recognized several of her own light blue envelopes. "None of these are opened. No one has been reading my reports." She picked up a handful. "Nanna, these could be important, my reports are important, what if Máni wrote or if the Fates had sent a prediction about the egg." Looking up from the stack in her hand, Nanna and Dahlia were now standing at the egg.

Now, Dahlia wore the ocular apparatus and looked from the surface of the egg to the large scroll in Nanna's hand.

Yggdrasil rolled her eyes. "Something in these piles could be about the egg and why it is on the verge of hatching at the Kolvandre stage." Nanna and Dahlia continued to ignore Yggdrasil. Yggdrasil too tired to think beyond the pile of correspondences plunked herself in front of them and started to open and organized them.

For the next three hours, Nanna and Dahlia went from egg to scrolls studying, Dogwood stoked the fire and added water and sulfur concoction to the cauldron, and Yggdrasil ripped open envelope after envelope finding nothing of importance except for an invitation to a ball from a new neighbor who wished to show off what he had done to a neighboring castle. The invite was four months old and the ball had already taken place.

The four of them dripped with the humidity as did the walls of the den. Yggdrasil mopped her brow and mumbled to herself, "Come on eureka moment before the paint peels off the den walls with all this humidity."

A stream of light pierced through the dankness, Mary, the cook, exclaimed, "Dear Thor! Are you trying to steam cook the dragon in its shell?"

Once Mary was through the door, Dogwood scrambled behind her and closed it, "I think I've finally achieved maximum humidity for the space. I don't want any vapors escaping." Yggdrasil watched his hurried scramble and couldn't believe his state. He was completely soaked through with sweat and covered with soot.

Mary stood, looking around the room. Yggdrasil took the tray from her, "Mary, it is good to see you. This looks delicious."

"I'm sorry not to have greeted you upon your arrival. The castle is in such a state, I barely look up from my work. I hope all this," Mary waved her hands around the room, "can be fixed." She left and took care not to open the door widely and closed it behind her.

Yggdrasil set the tray on the floor. "This is ridiculous. The stench, the heat and humidity and studying scrolls. The work Dahlia, Dogwood and I did out there made a difference and it didn't matter that I wrote it down, nothing could be repeated. No two things were the same. This egg is growing quickly and is not following the rules written down by someone hundreds of years ago. His writings don't matter. This is a different egg. Nanna is a different keeper of the egg. It's different, though, though...nothing changes."

She threw up her hands, stopped her tirade, and started to pace. Dogwood put more wood on the fire. Dahlia adjusted the ocular lenses' strength.

Nanna took a drink of water and watched Yggdrasil pace up and down the length of the egg four times. Then, like the water clearing her throat, Nanna's mind cleared. She walked to the windows and opened the curtains. Though the sun was almost complete set, the room lightened. "Dogwood, douse the fire and get rid of the contents of that cauldron. Dahlia, will you help me open the windows?"

Within minutes, the room completely changed. The air's darkness lifted. The gold flecks in the paint reflected light.

Dogwood, on his way back from dumping the cauldron, spotted a set of golden chairs and a table decorated with nymphs dancing in the wood. He brought it into the den.

Mary and the other two servants arrived with jugs of ale and more food. With everyone holding a full glass of the best ale, Nanna made a toast. "To Yggdrasil, Dahlia, and Dogwood, welcome back from your adventures."

Five days later, the castle remained nearly empty though hummed with spring type joy of impending new life. The egg continued to grow and changed since Nanna opened the curtains. She still spent most of her time with the egg singing and reading to it although now Nanna's joy shone like the wallpaper.

Yggdrasil, Dahlia, and Dogwood prepared the airship thinking their help was needed elsewhere.

Alice E Keyes grew up as a westerner in Montana. She loves the Rockies and is drawn to the open spaces and blue skies though she has always had bit of wanderlust. She has traveled through Europe, worked on a colonial replicated ship, and will be writing her next novel from Haiti. When she is not writing, she enjoys getting out into nature by either cycling or hiking.

http://aliceekeyes.blogspot.com

AFTER THE CRASH

B.A. SINCLAIR

THE FRAME OF THE DIRIGIBLE lay across the rocky plain like the bones of some great dinosaur. Scavengers had indeed taken what they could, to nearby caves, and in the log and earth homes they had built since the crash. Upon a nearby hill stood a log lookout tower. The watchmen had abandoned tending the wireless telegraph nearly two years ago when it became clear the outside world would not respond to their signals. Their job was now alerting the survivors to the approach of carnivores. Those in the tower experienced long periods of tedium, occasional excitement and sometimes terror. Today none of those emotions had been triggered. The day was clear and beautiful; the tower sunshade flapped in the warm breeze. Tara Marchinetti swept the entire plain and hills to the north with her binoculars as Thomas Elderson reached the top of the ladder and stepped onto the platform.

"Hi Tara," he said warmly.

"Thomas," replied Tara, curtly.

"Are you still angry with me, Tara?"

"That is correct, Mister Elderson." Tara slung her rifle over her shoulder and climbed down the ladder as fast as she could. Before she was one hundred steps from the tower, the alarm gong rang. Thomas was making an excuse to get her back up top.

"Elderson, you idiot," Tara said to herself. Frantic screaming from the tower made her look east. The plains grass was moving, and not due to the wind. She was already headed for the wreck of the MacTsaigart Lines airship Gold Dawn.

There was no time to ponder her fears. Tara began to sprint. She hoped that the attack was only by the mammalian carnivores that had tried to raid their camp before, and not something bigger. She risked a glance over her shoulder. The grass hiding the hungry beasts parted like a wave around a rock. They were much faster than she was. Thomas' rifle shots brought down several of the creatures, but the pack did not slow. The short-winged velociraptors cleared the grass, and having lost their cover, began short flying hops towards Tara. Ahead of her was the first trench, and the narrow footbridge, not much more than a plank. She could hear the velociraptors' hunting calls.

Crossing the bridge, she turned and kicked it into the spike filled trench. The carnivore nearest to her screamed, leapt, and fell, impaling itself on the wooden stakes. Tara ran on. She cleared the second row of trenches, and knocked the footbridge plank in.

Tara knelt and began to target the fierce dinosaurs. When her rifle bullets were spent, she pulled out her handgun, and fired until it was empty. Over one hundred of the creatures must have been in the initial charge. There must have been about twenty to thirty left. The things were smart. After several fell into the trenches and died, they stopped trying to jump across, but one more did slip and fall into the outer trench. It clambered over its dead fellows and ran to the edge of the inner defense, where it stood for a moment, and jumped in of its own volition. Unconcerned, Tara headed back to the dirigible. A scrabbling of claws on planks caused her to turn as the persistent velociraptor emerged. It flapped its short wings, and surged towards her. She barely had time to draw her sword. Tara plunged the tip of the blade into the beast's jaw and through the brain. It fell over dead. Grimacing she chopped off its head, and carried it back to the ruined airship.

Thaddeus March ambled up to her looking disgusted, followed by a worried looking Bettina Crawley.

"That could have been saved for science, girl."

"Thaddeus, you are a taxidermist," retorted Tara. Anything you get would be saved to sell, not for research. There's plenty more in the trenches. Feel free to retrieve your own." Thaddeus stomped out of the ruined dirigible.

"Do you have to be so abrasive to everyone?" asked Bettina.

"What difference would it make? They all still think the crash was my fault."

"Thomas does not. Neither do I."

Tara nodded, and carried the head to her cabins. Most of the gondola had been smashed, but the control room and a few of the rooms behind that had survived intact. Superstition or stupidity had kept everyone else from claiming the best residences in the makeshift village. Tara did not mind. She had become accustomed to living alone. Other than Thaddeus, Bettina and Thomas were the only people who talked to her regularly. Unfortunately, Thomas' amorous expressions had gone beyond tedium to presumption. Her friend Bettina had tried to become the village peacemaker, but had failed, and was now nearly as much of an outcast as the dirigible pilot. Tara placed the velociraptor head on her butcher block, which was merely a sawn stump. She began to pluck feathers off of the crest, placing them in a bowl to be washed. When she was about done, Thaddeus sauntered into her kitchen, and set something on the table.

"Dropped your knife out there," he said by way of explanation.

Tara glanced over at the table. "That is not my knife."

"It is now Tara. Good-bye." A quick glance at the blade showed that the abandoned weapon was worth keeping. The handle was strange, marked with deep scratches for decoration, perhaps. It definitely was not the work of someone in the village.

Tara encountered something very odd about the velociraptor head. Under the large crest of feathers was a bone projection. The protruding bone crest was covered in a contrivance that had a set of gears on the left side, and on the right a row of three small crystals, and a rotatable brass aperture which displayed a strange rune. She shrugged, dumped the head, device and all in a big pot of water to boil. The skull would adorn her trophy wall. The soup from the head could feed the semi-domesticated creatures in the village. Once the fire was started for the cook pot, Tara returned to the outer trench, to recover more dinosaur bodies. The villagers often left the worst of the jobs for her. Even Bettina did not join her. Thankfully Thomas was still on watchtower duty.

In retribution for lack of assistance Tara left twenty seven of the creatures between the defenses. Someone else would have to bring them past the inner trench, and butcher them. She noted that none of the rest of these bodies had an aethero-magical device. The adrenaline had worn off; she felt completely exhausted. Wobbling her way back to the dirigible wreck tired her further. Tara prepared a bath in her copper basin. When she was clean and changed, she washed her work clothes and hung them to dry.

"Tara! Tara Marchinetti!" Arthur Wyuts' voice was distinctive, thick with Dutch overtones. "May I come in?"

"Yes, Mr. Wyuts."

"Job's not done, Tara."

"Mr. Wyuts, I hauled nearly thirty velociraptor bodies. I cannot do any more today. And, sir, while you may have the greater sway over the villagers, having financed the voyage that brought us to this island, you are no-one's boss. Is that the only reason you are here? To badger me further?"

"Tara, sorry if that came across wrong. It's just that if you do as much as you can, it will go a long way with the survivors." He had actually apologized! Astonishing. "I've been talking to Bettina and understand things a bit differently now."

"Rather late, considering," said Tara. Wyuts' eyes flashed; he had lost his wife in the crash.

"I am sorry," said Tara. "My comment was not appropriate. I am sorry about your wife."

"Learn anything about the dinosaurs? We haven't seen that kind before."

"There was one odd thing; would you like to see?"

Wyuts nodded. Tara retrieved the skull, with the aethero-magical device still bonded to the skull. Wyut's eyebrows shot up.

"Any guesses, Tara, as to what that device is?"

"Something to exert control over the creature, or extend its intelligence, I suppose. In any case it means that someone has been meddling with these creatures longer than we have been stranded here."

Wyuts nodded, "Sounds like you've thought it through," he said, and left. Tara wondered whether he would share the information with others or keep it to himself. For some reason, she was uncomfortable with the thought that Thaddeus March or Thomas Elderson might learn of the altered dinosaur.

Tara now had a dog, Emilio, descended from canines that someone had smuggled aboard the dirigible. She supposed the reason the animal had selected her was the scent, from butchering and cooking the short wing velociraptors. In any case she now had a guard, and a dependent. To her amusement the dog growled whenever he saw Thomas Elderson. Thomas had made a joke about it, claiming that Tara had trained her dog to be hostile towards him. This was ludicrous. Tara had no time for such frivolity, nor for someone who professed to love her, and had hinted about, but not actually made a formal proposal of marriage.

Several days after the dinosaur attack, Tara had watchtower duty. Bettina was scheduled to follow her. Just before Bettina arrived, Arthur Wyuts rang the bell for a village meeting. Tara was quite displeased by the timing; she decided to skip the gathering, and pursue her plan to search for an explanation regarding the altered dinosaur. Bettina would tell her if anything of consequence was decided. When Bettina took the next watch, she eyed Tara's pack with great suspicion.

"Be careful, Tara. If the predators catch you…"

"They will kill me. I know. I'll use caution. The device on the velociraptor skull proves that someone has been on this island before. We need to learn what is going on."

She began her trek more motivated than she had been in three years. Tara followed a dinosaur she had spotted from the tower. Considering how fast the beasts could move, it was setting a lackadaisical pace. She did not believe it had sensed that she was tracking it. After about an hour the dinosaur stopped at a river. Tara hid behind a clump of bushes. The beast waded in and tilted its head, watching for movement beneath the surface. It dove. A second afterwards the dinosaur surfaced, a fish in its beak, and in each claw. Tara expected the beast to gobble the catch down immediately. What it did next astonished her. It tossed the fish onto leaves on the ground, then reached down with its right claw and withdrew a knife from a feather covered hip pouch. The dinosaur was an intelligent tool using creature! The creature deboned each fish, wrapped the pieces in a large leaf and placed them in the pouch. It scanned both banks of the river, then looked towards the trees, turning its head side to side, listening, and watching. Tara took in a sudden breath. The dinosaur turned its head quickly and began to walk towards where she was hidden. Tara panicked and ran. Though she had no hope of outrunning the knife-wielding velociraptor, still she ran.

From time to time she turned her head, hoping to hear whether her pursuer was closing. When should she turn and fight? Just ahead the river crossed her path; she had to turn south. With peripheral vision, she saw the creature loping along, keeping pace with her easily. She sprinted, hoping to see some means of escape. Instead directly ahead there loomed a rough wall of rocks and logs, built in a jumble, as if a beaver had tried to turn stonemason. She edged closer to the river bank, slipped and fell in. Flailing uselessly, she slid over a small waterfall, and plummeted into the large pool below. Tara hit her head on a rock and fell unconscious.

Tara awoke in the arms of a seven foot tall automaton. It strode along purposefully through country she hand never seen. She assessed the machine. Its iron skin had been fashioned to resemble a cut of men's apparel fashionable some fifty years earlier. A metal bowler had topped its head. Three eyes decorated an otherwise blank, round face. The metal man descended rough rock steps. Before her lay several acres of stone fenced land, with cultivated crops, and an array of enclosures, each holding a different breed of small dinosaur. As they reached the bottom step, the automaton set her down, and grasped her by the left forearm. The thing walked at a slower pace. She was thankful she did not have to run; her head hurt a lot. They approached one of the fenced paddocks along which lay some small log and stone houses. The metal man stopped, inclined its head towards her as if to say *'stay put.'*

It reached in through a hatch, withdrew two chickens, and threw them into the fenced yard. Seven small dinosaurs emerged from a hut in the center. Tara noticed that aethero-magical devices that ran from the top of their skulls down their necks. The contrivances were similar to the one on the skull in her kitchen, but more elaborate, with several sets of gears, and three to five brass apertures each showing unusual runes. The creatures devoured the chickens in seconds, then approached the metal machine-man, screeching for attention. The dinosaur-keeper placed a heavy hand on her shoulder. The machine emitted a low, pulsing thrum sound. The creatures lined up, single file, and approached the wall where Tara stood. Each dinosaur executed an elaborate dance. Not knowing what else to do, she acknowledged their efforts with a slight bow.

When the exchange was complete, the automaton grasped her arm, and pulled her along until they reached a cave. The entrance was sealed with an iron door. Nearby an artificial stream had been dug, fed by the river. This culminated in a rocky pool, from which jutted colorful crystals. In the center of the water, sat an open eight sided metal frame supported by stone pillars. It looked like a crude electrostatic protection cage. The automaton opened the cave door and pulled Tara inside. The machine made itself busy for a time, then brought her a wooden plate, with cooked fish, root vegetables, and a mug with fresh stream water. The automaton receded to the back of the cave. Tara glanced about looking for something to keep her occupied. A stack of dusty books sat on a table, with a chair nearby. She swept the dust from the chair, and picked up the top book. "Eidechese-Schmitt Experiment," declared the cover page. The first several pages were filled with rather fine sketches of native dinosaurs, crystals, and an automaton similar to her captor. Finally she found an explanation.

"Season of Rains, Day the Seventeenth: The automatons are performing better than expected. This is fortunate, because most of the other scientists are dead. Some have succumbed to unknown diseases, or attacks by our modified dinosaurs. Our means of control is clearly not yet sufficient."

She leafed many pages ahead, skipping the excellent sketches, eager for more information.

"Season of Migration, Day the Forty Fifth: This shall be my last entry. I am dying. Only one automaton remains, the one in the bowler hat. He has all of the required information to proceed with the experiment, and the design for a new control belt, well, corset actually. We speculate that the

modified dinosaurs will respond better to a lady than a gentleman. Time will tell.

Faithfully yours,

Jerimiah Wyutts

Tara found an old satchel and tucked the logbook inside. About an hour later the mechanical man reappeared, dragging a small, chained dinosaur along behind. It struggled ineffectively. Suddenly it rushed forward, and bit its captor on the leg. It left a couple of minor scratches, and a broken tooth on the cave floor. The door slammed shut. Tara walked quickly to the portal, lifted the latch and peeked out. The dinosaur had been placed in the metal frame. On its neck was a metal collar, which was chained to an iron pole at the very center. On its head was a metal cap. It squawked and yammered until exhausted. The automaton reached for a rock, and pushed the top back, revealing a hollow chamber containing a series of levers, and dials. As it worked the control panel, aethero-magical energy surged from the crystals in the pool to the wrought iron cage. The little dinosaur howled and surged futilely against the chain. This routine continued for a week. Though Tara could see no physical changes in the creature, day by day its behavior changed. It ceased its protests and became more alert, more attentive, seemingly more intelligent.

The seventh day after her incarceration, the automaton presented her with a corset that looked as if inspired by a medieval plaque belt, panels adorned alternately with runes and set gems. Clearly the machine wanted her to put the garment on. She could see no reason not to do so, and took the elaborate contrivance from the machine man. She wrapped the thing around her waist, and closed the clasps. The automaton walked to the cave door, and beckoned her to follow it outside. Tara grabbed the satchel which held the logbook and followed the automaton.

They walked to a glade in the center of which was a roughly circular platform, surrounded by seven smaller flat stones, just big enough to stand on. It uttered a low thrum, and pointed at Tara to stand on the central stone. Cautiously she stepped up. The automaton abandoned her for a few minutes. She considered running, but suspected that the metal man could easily chase her down. The clanking creature reappeared followed by seven small dinosaurs. What was going on here? Tara thought about the chickens from several days ago. She watched the creatures step onto the smaller surrounding stones. They craned their necks, and looked at her with curiosity. She was in her element at the helm of a dirigible, not with a strange mechanical caretaker of laboratory experiment dinosaurs. The automaton placed a series of aethero-magical devices around her.

As each was set in place, the machine man thrummed, and the dinosaurs sang. The sun set. Light from the mechanisms illuminated the glade. An aperture opened on each device, and shone on her corset. Tara looked down at her waist. Each gem, and each rune had lit up. Her fingertips and toes, then her forearms, the core of her body, the nape of her neck, and skull began to tingle. Abruptly her mind began to race, as if in the days following the dirigible crash trying to sleep, but unable to quell her thoughts, rehashing the final moments of the flight, searching for what she might have done differently to save the ship, save their way off the island. She thought she had been done with such worries. Why were these memories intruding now? Again the automaton intoned its commands to the dinosaurs; they stepped off their little stones and approached her. Was this now the end? If so, why the theatre and the aethero-magical effects? As one the creatures bowed to her, skilled as any courtier of old. Not knowing what else to do, she bowed in return. The automaton gestured as if to say, *"you are free to go."* She waited a moment longer. The metal man gestured again.

"Very well," said Tara. She looked at the reptiles crowded around her, gazing at her in expectation. "What do you want of us?" The automaton again signaled that she should leave.

"Troops," said Tara to the seven dinosaurs, "your metal creator desires that we leave. Let's go." She made a shooing motion with both hands. They crowded closer, big eyes staring at her. Tara began to walk out of the glade. The seven creatures made excited cries, and rushed to follow. She looked back at the automaton, who raised an iron hand in farewell. The dinosaurs spread out around her, and became silent and serious. Their heads moved about, alert for danger. They set out across country. She led the group to a plain with thick grasses varying from knee to chest height. To her right lay rocky hills and scrubby trees. She preferred to cross on the easier path, rather than clamber through the sharp rocks to the north. The dinosaurs held back, unsure.

She saw the gears on their metal skull plates begin to turn, and different runes show in the brass apertures. She had assumed the gears on the back of her corset were ornamental, but felt and heard clicking as the mechanism began to move. What was going on? Two of her charges stood beside her, craning their necks, and putting their short snouts in the air. The other five had crowded rather closely in front of her protectively. Some distance ahead of them, the grass began to move. The attacking creature emitted a series of grunts and squeals. The dinosaurs standing beside her each held a claw outstretched. An oblong green glow suddenly appeared on each fore-limb, then fired towards the charging animal. A pained grunt met Tara's ears; a hideous pig-like beast fell in front of her. Bony plates stood out from each jaw. A plethora of tusks jutted randomly from its mouth and massive head. She expected that her seven dinosaurs would begin to feast right away. Instead they approached the body and sniffed, then stepped away disdainfully. The beast began to breathe in pained intakes. Two of the dinosaurs gently put claws on her arm and led her away, then stopped, looking at her for guidance.

To the south Tara spotted three tall carnivorous dinosaurs. She pointed at the rocks to the north and said, "Maybe the hills would be better."

They began to move with determination away from the carnivores and dying pig-beast. More squealing began as the large dinosaurs began to hunt. By then Tara and her group of augmented dinosaurs were safely in the rocks. The landscape resembled that of the hills north of the village. They travelled way west. Before nightfall she spotted the watchtower. She crouched down behind some large rocks, and signaled her dinosaurs to do the same. "I cannot take you into the village. They would not understand. The people would kill you all. You will have to stay outside."

They all blinked and stared at her. Tara threw her hands up in frustration and said sternly, "Stay away!"

The creatures all looked sad. Their headpiece gears turned; the rune apertures spun through several symbols. One by one the dinosaurs put their claws on her arms, signaling farewell.

"Hunt. Be stealthy. Be safe," she admonished her dinosaurs, hoping they would at least understand her tone. Tara walked through the grass, and passed by the watchtower, either unnoticed, or ignored. Her transit across the plank footbridges was quick and quiet. She went to her rooms. Tara took off the corset, and looked it over carefully. The logbook entry had indicated that the device was made by the mechanical man. She examined the runes and gems carefully, then flipped it over to assess the gear mechanism on the back. She had a sudden thought, and walked to her boiling pot, but the dinosaur head was gone. Who had taken it? Perhaps the dog had gotten into the pot. The skull should be lying about somewhere. She searched every room, but found nothing. She had a sudden chill along her back. Arthur Wyutts was the only person in the village to whom she had mentioned that there was something strange about the dinosaur head. Perhaps he had broken in while she was gone. Well, there was no way to compare the workings of the corset with the dead dinosaur's headpiece now.

She spent the next two weeks getting back to her usual routine, and experimenting with the aethero-magical corset.

At daybreak Tara heard the sounds of a violent argument. She grabbed her sword and pistol and ran outside. Arthur Wyutts lay on the ground dead. The satchel from the automaton's cave was beside him, empty. Tara looked around. Thaddeus March and Thomas Elderson were headed towards the watchtower. Tara edged towards the inner ditch, busying herself with an apparent inspection of the trap covers. The two men stopped briefly to talk to Bettina on watch, then ambled off over the hill. Tara sprinted for the tower, then followed their trail. She managed to keep them in view without being seen. They made their way to a rocky hillside, and into a cave. Tara managed to climb the hill above it, and lay down, trying to keep out of sight and listen to the conversation.

"The Eidechese-Schmitt experiment is a complete failure," said Thaddeus March disgustedly. "The replica automaton had few of the capabilities reported of the originals.

"That was not entirely surprising," said Thomas Elderson, "we knew there were issues even before the airship began its voyage here."

"Never mind that," said Thaddeus, "Tara has become too curious. Thomas, you said you would deal with her. Do so."

"Do not be concerned. I will bend her to my will."

"Failing that, you shall have to kill her."

"Agreed."

Tara felt a sudden fear, as if being hunted by some predatory dinosaur. Although she certainly did not like Thomas, and had maintained only a surface civility with Thaddeus, she would not previously have thought either of them capable of homicide. She edged back from the hilltop, and ran through the woods. She hurried through the tall grass that surrounded their village, and climbed the watchtower ladder.

"Whatever is the matter, Tara?" asked Bettina.

"Thomas Elderson intends to murder me," declared Tara. She waited for Bettina's reaction.

"Are you certain of this, Tara? I thought Thomas adored you."

"I heard them talking, and Arthur Wyutts was killed this morning."

"Who was talking? Who killed Mr. Wyutts?"

"The two that went over the hill. Thaddeus and Thomas. If you see or hear anything unusual, please let me know," said Tara. Her friend nodded.

"Of course. I do not want you in further danger."

Tara headed back to the village, and hurried to the dirigible frame. Emilio greeted her excitedly. The dirigible pilot sat down at her kitchen table, chin on hands, and stared at the corset with its now familiar aethero-magical device. She considered her options. Declaring what she had just overheard to the rest of the village would lead to further ostracism. Elderson and March would simply claim that it was she who had murdered Arthur Wyutts. No one would believe her. She hopped up, fastened the corset around her torso, and grabbed her pistol and rifle. It was time to find her dinosaurs.

After nightfall Tara crossed the spike filled trenches. She stopped and studied the watchtower. The guard actually seemed to be asleep. Emilio came charging after her. "Daft dog!" she scolded quietly, glancing back at the tower. Somewhere from the south came the sound of a screaming predator. The dog slunk along beside her. She headed towards Elderson's cave. Along the way Emilio began to bark excitedly. Tara readied the only weapon she had found in the corset's mechanisms, and drew her pistol. One of her dinosaurs appeared.

"Where are the others?" Tara asked and spread her arms wide, hoping that the gesture would convey meaning to the augmented animal. It gave a low whistle, and the six other little dinosaurs appeared, looking at her expectantly.

"Time for a little exploration," she said, and strode forward purposefully. Emilio, however, caused a momentary distraction. The dinosaurs could not decide if he was dinner, or a friend. Tara grabbed his collar. "These are my assistants," she said to the dog in calm, soothing tones. They will not hurt you; do not antagonize them."

Emilio took to her tone, but walked very close to her, tail down as they moved on to Elderson's cave. At the entrance she listened for conversation. Hearing nothing, she entered, weapons at the ready, followed by her dinosaur and canine retinue. Gas lamps were burning brightly throughout the cave. Five comfortable chairs salvaged from the dirigible were set in a semi-circle. At the back of the cave was a large metal door, which certainly had not come from the airship. It looked old, worn, rusty in places, but still functional.

"What has Thomas Elderson been up to?" wondered Tara. She pulled the door's lever and swung it open. She hefted her pistol, checked the rifle sling. They began a slow careful walk down a sloping spiral stone corridor. After twenty minutes or so, the tunnel finally opened out onto a gallery, stretching to the left and right. She got her bearings quickly. To the east lay a set of stones, looking almost like...

"Tombstones!" exclaimed Tara, and hurried to read the carvings. "Captain Reginald Bennet, First Mate Harald Kaneq..."

"Pilot Tara Marchinetti!" exclaimed Thomas Elderson, "I was so hoping we would not have to add your name to one of the blank stones."

Thaddeus stood behind him, brandishing a weapon. "But look ... you have been exploring, and acquiring! The corset suits you, Tara. Your lizard companions. I must ask how you did it. Quite impressive. We all thought you were simply a dirigible pilot, a hapless dupe. It was all too easy to scuttle the dirigible and lay the blame on you. Now, remove the corset, drop the weapons, and order your pets to be docile."

Emilio began to growl and slowly stepped in front of Tara. "No, dog. Sit."

Astonishingly, Emilio did as ordered. To buy a bit of time, Tara dropped the pistol, carefully unslung the rifle and set it on the ground. With her right hand, she reached for the first corset fastening, but with her left, she made a fist, and willed the weapon to do its job. Instantly the dinosaurs followed suit. Together they unleashed a series of green aethero-magical energies at the conspirators. Thaddeus March fell. Elderson did not.

Thomas laughed. "Did you think I had not done my research?"

Tara and her dinosaurs fired a second wave of magic. With one hand Thomas reached out and absorbed the energies aimed at him. With the other he emitted a beam that swept across the dinosaurs. Tara heard some of them fall. She felt the gears at the back of her corset whirling madly. Tara tried to send another burst of the aethero-magical stunning power at Thomas. Nothing happened. He swept his attacking beam across her body, but she felt only a dull ache. Perhaps the corset was protecting her.

Thomas began to raise both hands in one last triumphant gesture of attack, then looked confused when no energy blasted forth. Tara reached for the rifle as Thomas ran at her. Having no time to aim, she brought the rifle barrel up into his gut. He let out a "whoof" and pitched forward, falling behind her. The remaining four dinosaurs stood around his prone form menacingly, jaws working, headpiece gears turning madly. Thaddeus was still unconscious. Three of Tara's dinosaurs were dead.

"We are heading back to the village, Thomas. Do not cause any trouble, or I will set my dinosaurs upon you."

Elderson walked along maintaining a docile attitude. When they arrived, Tara rang the village assembly bell.

"Tara is here with her deadly creatures to finish you all!" shouted Thomas desperately.

"Silence, man!" hissed Tara. Emilio rushed forward and bit him on the leg. "Watch him," said Tara to her dinosaurs.

Tara looked out over the assembled villagers. "Re-introductions are in order. This is Thomas Elderson, conspirator, and saboteur of our airship," she said loudly. "Lock him away. I am Tara Marchinetti, dirigible pilot, master of dinosaurs, and wielder of aethero-magics." She looked at the dirigible wreck, and back to the people in front of her. "It is time to re-build the airship, and time for us to leave this land."

B.A. Sinclair has an education in metallurgy, and is employed as an engineer. He writes steampunk, science fiction and fantasy. He is currently working on "Eliza McIntire and the Iron Horse." When not reading or writing, he studies renaissance swordplay.

ACKNOWLEDGEMENTS

Jack Tyler would like to thank the members of Scribblers' Den for taking the time to create these wonderful stories, and Bryce Raffle for his diligent work in bringing them together in this volume.

Bryce Raffle would like to thank his fellow denizens for their efforts, support, and advice. And thanks to Jack Tyler for his efforts in establishing Scribblers' Den and keeping it afloat.

David Lee Summers would like to thank the members of the Scribblers' Den for ongoing support and inspiration, Kumie Wise for believing in jackalopes, and Maggie Bonham who provides the literary home for most of Marshal Larissa Seaton's adventures through her company, Sky Warrior Book Publishing.

Steve Moore would like to thank The Baroness herself, JML Carlson of New England, USA, Bryce Raffle of Vancouver, Canada and the mysterious Dark Lady of his dreams.

B.A. Sinclair would like to thank Bryce Raffle for his diligent efforts on this anthology, and to Jack Tyler (Blimprider) for creating Scribblers' Den, challenging us to write more and better steampunk.

William J. Jackson would like to thank Jack Tyler and the Scribblers' Den for their friendship and heartfelt support, and the readers of Den of Antiquity.

N.O.A. Rawle would like to thank Scribblers' Den members for their support with her forays into writing steampunk and their patience with her editing.

www.ingramcontent.com/pod-product-compliance
Lightning Source LLC
Chambersburg PA
CBHW072137170626
46813CB00004BA/1596